SNOW WHITE AND THE SEVEN ROGUES

WOLF SHIFTER FAIRY TALE RETELLINGS
BOOK FIVE

BELLA MOONDRAGON

For Nikki. Thanks for having my back.

CONTENTS

1

ROYAL BLOOD

The blood moon rises bright and scarlet over the treetops, staining the sky with a deep crimson glow. Its light washes over me as if it knows my name, as if it recognizes that this is the moment I have been preparing for since the day I was born. Tonight is my twenty-first birthday. Tonight, I take the oath that will bind me to the Moonfang Pack forever–as the only living blood heir in my father's lineage.

I stand at the center of the stone courtyard, surrounded by torches that light up the winter night. Pack members crowd around the outer circle, their faces lifted toward me with expectation and pride.

"Xamara," Beta Branok calls, his voice carrying like rolling thunder. "Daughter of Alpha Blood. Last of the Moonfang Line. Step forward."

I obey, each footfall reverberating through the powerful, ancient stones. The wind picks up, carrying the scent of pine and fire and the electric promise of transformation. I lift my chin, meeting Branok's eyes as he holds the Moonstone Tear, an iridescent, opal-blue drop of stone given only to royal heirs on this special night.

Branok raises the Moonstone Tear with both hands, his expression solemn as he brings it toward my face. The stone warms as it nears my skin, its light blooming brighter. When he sets it gently between my eyebrows, a cool ribbon of energy unfurls through me, curling down my spine, stirring my wolf awake in a way I have never felt before. The gathered warriors and villagers watch as the stone settles, glowing in perfect rhythm with my pulse.

"Tonight," he continues, "you come into your power. You honor the promise of your ancestors, whose magic once united wolf and man. Do you swear to lead with strength, to protect without fear, and to uphold the sacred bond of the Moonfang?"

"I swear," I say.

Branok holds a blade to my palm. I feel a sting, a bead of blood, and then the power of the Moon Goddess fills me. I feel it rush through me in a white-hot surge, flooding my limbs, my chest, and my lungs. For a moment, I can't breathe. The moon blazes above me, and the pack howls, their voices rising in harmony. Power bursts beneath my skin, radiating through me and rearranging, as if trying to remember where it belongs.

When the rush finally settles, I lift my head. The world looks sharper and brighter, and every sound and movement around me snaps into perfect focus.

I am no longer just Xamara. I am the only heir of the last blood Alpha of Moonfang Pack, and my wolf is very near.

The crowd erupts. Shifter warriors howl, elders raise their hands in blessing, and children beam with curious pride.

Someone presses a goblet into my hand, filled with warm, spiced, sweet berry wine, and the music begins. The drums beat first. Then, strings join in, and voices swirl in the deep, rolling chant that belongs only to us. Women dance near the fire pit, their skirts swaying with the embers in the breeze. Pack members grab me, laughing, pulling me into the celebration, and I let myself be swept into it.

I enjoy the moment, the cheers, the warmth, the strange new power humming under my ribs. Wolves shift around the edges of the courtyard, howling up at the blood moon in my honor. Plates of roasted elk, honey cakes, and fruit are passed around. Everywhere I look, there is light, joy, and pride.

And then there is Luna Selvara. My stepmother stands near the royal table, her expression smooth as carved marble. She smiles when our eyes meet, but there is something off about it. Her mask of expressions are too practiced, too polite. I've lived with her long enough to know the difference between affection and performance. She raises her goblet in a way that anyone who didn't know her would think was sincere. I return the gesture.

As the celebration deepens, the wolves grow louder and wilder. Eventually, when the food is picked through and the music softens, Luna Selvara stands. Her voice rings out above the crowd's laughs and murmurs.

"Warriors of Moonfang," she calls, "a patrol is needed along the southern border. The woods grow restless on nights of the blood moon. I want a full team checking the outer perimeter."

The announcement cuts through the festivities. Warriors exchange looks but obey quickly. No one refuses a Luna, especially not this one.

When the last echoes of music fade, replaced by the murmurs of goodnights, and the crowd thins, the blood moon still guards overhead, pulsing in time with the new power stirring in my veins. I feel restless. My skin tingles, and my bones ache as though something beneath them is waiting, stretching, and preparing.

I step away from the courtyard and through the tree line. The forest seems to open for me, shadows parting, branches leaning as though recognizing my lineage. My breath quickens. The pull to my wolf grows stronger, like an ancient instinct calling me forward.

And then my body answers.

Heat rushes through me, bending my spine, reshaping muscle and bone. I fall to my knees as my vision fractures and then sharpens. Fur bursts along my arms, then my back, soft, pale, and luminous. A low cry escapes me, half-pain, half-awed disbelief, and as the shift completes, I stand on four legs.

My fur is snow white, reflecting pink beneath the blood moon's red cast. For a heartbeat, I simply breathe, overwhelmed by new senses flooding in: the feel of the earth beneath my paws, the crispness of every scent, the whisper of wind threading through branches miles away.

Instinct takes over, and I run. The forest blurs around me, dark trunks, silver leaves, and streaks of moonlit ground. I weave between trees with a grace I never knew I possessed. Every bound feels like flying. Every breath tastes clean.

Then—I freeze.

A metallic tang hits my nose, sharp and wrong. Blood. Fresh blood.

My ears snap forward. My heart thunders harder as I lift my snout and inhale deeper. The scent trails through the underbrush, winding south, curling around the roots like an invitation–or a warning.

Without hesitation, I follow the scent. Curiosity and the power of my first shift drives me deeper into the woods. Something, or someone, is bleeding, and they might need help.

As I creep forward, each pawstep sinking silently into the frost-hardened earth, the scent of blood grows more pronounced with every stride, thickening the air until it settles heavy on my tongue and makes my stomach clench. Something strange is woven into its coppery bite, something tainted and unnatural that sets every instinct inside me on edge. The cold deepens as I enter a denser stretch of trees, and the shadows between their trunks seem to sway even though the wind has stilled completely.

Through the branches, I see swift, distorted movement. Every instinct tells me this is all wrong. My muscles tighten in readiness, but the shapes above the ground move in ways no wolf or human ever could. A faint rustle sweeps across the treetops, followed by a low, rhythmic thrum like wings pushing through the air. Snow drifts from shaken branches and spirals in pale bursts around me. I tilt my head upward, my eyes narrowing as I search for the source of the sound, and the moonlight finally reveals them.

Not wolves. Not bats. Not anything I have ever been told stories about.

Their bodies twist with a grotesque horror as they descend in slow, hovering arcs, their limbs long and sinewy like the stretched shadows of demons. Their wings beat with a leathery whisper that makes my fur stand on end. I catch glimpses of faces half-hidden by the night. They have angular cheekbones, elongated canines, and eyes gleaming like molten rubies. Some have tufts of fur along their arms and shoulders, while others have bare patches of scaled skin or clawed fingers that curl and uncurl as though testing the air, searching for me. They look like they've been fused together from different beasts–in ways that feel deliberate rather than accidental, as if they were shaped by something ancient and merciless.

Before me, bodies dot the ground. Wolves are sprawled in unnatural angles, their fur matted, and the earth is blood-soaked beneath. My stomach churns as I count familiar patrol members. This is the patrol Selvara just sent out, and whatever these winged abominations are, they found them first and tore through them like they were nothing.

The first shriek cuts through the night. It's not the cry of a creature defending territory but the sound of hunger, sharp and desperate. More join in, screaming in a dark melody that vibrates through my bones. My legs tense in reflexive preparation to leap, but the nearest creature swoops lower, its wings stirring the air around me. Its scent hits me. It's a sickly mixture of rot, dark magic, and cold blood, and I know instantly that whatever these things are, they have nothing to do with my pack or any pack sworn to the Moon Goddess.

Another shriek rings out overhead, and instinct takes control before rational thought has time to catch up. I bolt deeper into the forest, weaving through tangled roots and brittle underbrush as the creatures follow in fluid, terrifying silence broken only by those intermittent cries. The wind from their wings lashes the back of my neck as they dive and rise again, playing with their prey rather than striking. My breath steams in rapid bursts, my heart hammering so hard that it feels like it might jump out of my chest, but I keep running because slowing would mean death.

The deeper I go, the stranger the woods become. The moonlight turns glassy, fractured, as though filtered through invisible veils of spellwork. Behind me, the creatures shriek again, louder, and I almost stumble from the way the sound rattles in my ears. I push myself harder, paws pounding the ground in frantic rhythm, lungs burning from the cold and exertion. I leap over a fallen trunk and crash through a curtain of low branches, desperate to put distance between myself and whatever hunts me. But the forest has become unfamiliar, the land twisted into strange, mirrored versions of themselves.

I break into a clearing that I have never seen before. The snow here glows faintly as though lit from beneath, and the trees curve inward, branches arching like rib bones over an altar. My paws skid across the icy ground as I try to change direction, but a sudden blast of frigid wind forces me to brace myself. One of the creatures descends to the edges of the clearing, circling in slow patterns, wings stirring loose snow into a swirling halo that traps me.

My pulse thunders as they hover, watching me with those red, gleaming eyes. Their expressions twist into shapes that could only mean cruelty. The forest feels sealed around us, the night heavy and hostile, and every instinct screams that I must keep moving if I want to live.

I lower my body, muscles coiled, white fur bristling beneath the blood moon's pulse. The creatures close in, their shrieks rising again.

And I run... not because I know where I'm going, but because stopping means certain death.

2

BATTLE UNDER THE BLOOD MOON

Snow explodes beneath my paws as I run, my lungs burning, my muscles screaming. The forest whips past in streaks of black shadows and white drifts. I can barely feel my legs anymore, but I keep pushing because the creatures behind me will not stop. They don't tire. They don't slow. They only shriek, fly, swoop, and claw.

Their shadows sweep over the treetops, warped shapes that blot out the blood moon. Its crimson light should spill across the forest, but every time they pass overhead, it's swallowed whole, plunging the world into a sudden, unnatural darkness that sinks all the way into my bones.

I leap over a fallen trunk, land hard, skid, and keep going. My breath is a ragged cloud that rips from my chest. I can hear them above me, the beating of wings too large and heavy to be natural. They circle and dive with purpose as though they are made by black magic and hunger.

One shriek cuts through the night, sharp enough to pierce through my skull. I flatten my ears and throw myself forward faster. Snow blasts upward behind me as something slams into the ground, too close this time. I feel the vibration through my paws.

I veer left, weaving between trees, trying to break their line of sight. My paw catches on a buried root. I stumble and nearly fall. Pain flashes up my leg, but I force myself upright before the next shadow drops.

Another dive. The rush of air skims along my back, cold as ice slicing through fur. I twist mid-stride, barely dodging talons that carve lines across the snow where I just stood. A low growl scrapes out of my throat, instinctive and weak. I'm tiring, but I can't let up.

I push forward, and the trees betray me where they thin. Moonlight spills onto open snow, which is deadly. I'm exposed with nowhere to hide. I skid to a stop for half a second, panting, my heart punching against my ribs. Behind me, the forest erupts with another shriek. I have no choice. I bolt into the clearing.

My paws pound against the snow, too loud, too slow. Shadows ripple over me. One creature dives. The impact of its passing knocks me sideways. I roll, snow filling my nose and mouth. Before I rise, claws rake across my shoulder like fire, tearing through my flesh. I yelp and stagger upright, hot blood meeting the freezing air.

The forest waits ahead. I lunge toward it, stumbling more than running now. My injured leg drags, and all the heat leaves my trembling body.

Another dive. I drop to my belly, instinct taking over, but this time my limbs don't push me up fast enough. I try once, twice, my muscles shake violently and fail. Snow presses cold and unforgiving against my chest.

I lift my head just enough to see the tree line sway. My breaths come shallow as the blood from my leg melts the snow beneath me, my strength slipping away with it.

A larger, closer shadow descends. I bare my teeth weakly as it drops over me, and then my body gives out completely, sinking into the snow.

I hold my breath, waiting the final blow. The ground shakes under the weight of something large heading in my direction. More of the monsters? Or something else?

Several wolves explode out of the trees, massive bodies ripping through the shadows with shocking speed. Snow bursts under their paws as they split into formation with practiced instinct, teeth bared, low snarls rolling through the clearing.

A huge dark-furred wolf, broad as a boulder, slams into one of the creatures mid-dive, his jaws snapping its wing clean off. The creature shrieks, thrashes once, and then crumbles into drifting ash before it even hits the ground.

A blond wolf, smaller and quicker, darts past me in a blur. He moves with sharp, clever precision, circling and baiting. Every movement is calculated as he draws one in, and then his teeth flash, tearing into the creature's throat. More ash scatters across the snow.

Three female wolves flank my sides, weaving around me in tight arcs, fast and coordinated. The lavender one is sleek and silent as a shadow, while the copper female is sharp-eyed and poised. They strike in synchronized lunges. The quieter, honey-colored wolf moves so lightly she barely disturbs the snow. She leaps high enough to rip a creature straight from the air.

A silver wolf barrels through next, hot-headed and reckless, roaring a growl that vibrates through the clearing. He crashes into a bat twice his size, slamming it into a tree so hard the trunk splinters. The creature dissolves into ash under his paws.

They're rogues, but they're fighting like they've done this together for years.

Three more bats dive from the treetops, and the giant wolf, the one who led the charge, blocks the first with his whole body, his teeth sinking into the monster's skull before it can claw him. It folds into ash around him.

A chestnut wolf cleverly darts away and calls out with a short, urgent bark, like he's giving orders. The blond male beside him answers with a growl, switching positions and bracing for the next attack. Their coordination is strategic, instinctive, and incredibly fierce. And then everything narrows because the winged beasts that are left are still focused on *me*.

Four of the winged monsters drop at once, shrieking, wings beating the snow into spirals. They slam onto my back, my side, and my legs. Claws dig through fur and straight into flesh. More blood spills down my ribs. I snarl and twist, but I'm already too weak. My limbs buckle. The snow opens under me like a pit as they drag me down.

A massive weight crashes into the pile. My eyes are slits, but I can see it's the black wolf. He tears the closest creature off me with brutal strength, shaking it until it bursts into ash. The reckless silver wolf lunges at another, ripping its wing free with a furious snap.

The copper female strikes with sharp precision, dragging the third monster off my hind legs, pinning it, shredding it into ash.

The last creature clings to my shoulder, its claws piercing deep. I can't push myself up anymore. Pain shoots down my spine.

The lavender rogue dives in from behind, biting the creature's neck and wrenching it away from me. It dissolves before her paws touch the ground.

A stillness settles over the clearing as ash drifts like black snow around us. The rogues form a loose circle around me, panting and watching the skies for another wave of monsters.

I try to stand, but my legs fold, and my vision spins. Their paws blur into streaks of silver, black, and red. My vision is swimming. I can no longer focus.

I've lost too much blood. A low, commanding growl vibrates near my ear. Without looking, I know it's the giant wolf, the leader. He nudges my shoulder, firm but careful, urging me to move. One of them lets out a sharp, worried bark.

The forest dims. I try to lift my head and to stay conscious, but darkness pulls harder, and my body gives out completely.

Everything goes dark.

3

NIGHTBORN

The fire burns low in the courtyard. My Beta Mason sits in front of me. The castle looms behind, while shadows flicker in the light.

"I'm going to try to track the Nightborn tomorrow morning," I say.

"Will you be going alone, or do you want me there with you?" Mason asks.

"No, I'll go alone. It'll be easier to remain unscented and unseen."

"Understood," Mason nods. "I'll keep watch here while you're gone."

"I'll report what I find in the morning," I say. "We'll have a meeting when I get back."

Mason nods. "I'll round everyone up. We'll be ready."

As the fire dies to embers, and the whiskey is drained to its last drops, we discuss how the warriors should handle such a ferocious enemy. By midnight, the blood moon is high overhead, and Mason heads down the lane toward his home while I slip back inside the castle.

When I return to my chambers, I step out onto the balcony and look up at the night sky. I think about the monsters who've been invading my territory. By morning, they could tear through some of my livestock, or worse, some of my people. I let the thought run through my mind, planning what I'll need to do at sunrise. We don't know enough about the beasts to strike yet, but I will find them, learn their secrets, and end their wrath.

DAWN CREEPS SLOWLY OVER THE GLEABHAIN RIVER VALLEY, ITS PALE gold light filtering through the lingering mist in thin, wavy sheets. I run the ridge at a quick, ground-eating pace, my paws gripping the icy earth as the cold air rushes past my muzzle. The world smells sharper at this hour–the tang of the river, the deep resin of pine, the faint musk of deer bedding somewhere beyond the hills. It should be a peaceful morning, the kind that settles my Alpha instincts and reminds me why I protect this land with every breath I take, but peace has been rare these past weeks, and guilt flows through me with every stride.

The birds should already be waking, calling to one another across the valley. Instead, the forest sits unnervingly still. The silence isn't natural. Someone or something is watching, causing this uncomfortable calm.

Reports from the outer hunters through the mind-link churn through my mind, each one worse than the last. Livestock has been torn apart with precision and bodies left bloodless. Horses were found collapsed beside the river, their throats marked with strange punctures. My hunters return shaken and pale, claiming to have seen shadows with wings gliding above the treetops. Even the most seasoned scouts struggle to describe the creatures, their voices quivering, their tones laced with terror. I want to believe they are exaggerating, that fear made monsters out of mist, but the wounds I inspect tell a different story.

Something is here. Something bold enough to toy with us. Too bold a threat becomes an enemy.

My paws slip into the shallows of the Gleabhain River as I descend the slope, icy water splashing against my fur. The shock is intense, awakening my every sense. The current swirls around my legs, carrying scents from miles upriver. I sift through them as only a wolf can, separating the layers until one faint thread curls upward and hits me like a shard of cold metal.

It must be the creatures' scent—faint, new, and undeniable. They're not something born of this valley or any nearby territory. They're a strange blend of feral notes, laced with blood, with an undercurrent reminiscent of rot held in the black magic hands of something even darker, crueler, and colder. It coils in the air like a warning, too dangerous to ignore, and it makes my hackles rise.

I lift my head, scanning the tree line. The mist hangs heavy, shrouding half the forest in a dim blur, but even through it, I can sense the imbalance. The deer that should be grazing in the meadow haven't emerged. No squirrels chatter from the branches. No owls sweep into their nests. The forest is bracing itself, and that knowledge tightens the muscles along my spine.

I move upriver at a slow trot. My pawsteps are silent against the damp ground, my senses stretched thin. I know every bend of this river, every path carved by animals and storms alike. I know where danger should come from—and where it should not. I came to the forest alone deliberately so as to be the perfect bait for the predators.

I am halfway around a curve in the riverbank when the wind changes direction suddenly. It's not a natural breeze. It's an unnerving displacement.

A shadow drifts across the mist. I freeze, my claws digging into the earth. The hair along my back lifts as I tilt my head, narrowing my eyes against the pale sunrise. I see it weaving high above the trees.

For a moment, I think it's a large bird, but the silhouette moves strangely. Its wings are long and narrow, the joints bending in ways that turn my gut. The body beneath them is too broad for any ordinary creature, almost human-shaped, though stretched unnaturally thin. It glides in silence, not beating its wings but hovering, controlled. I lower myself instinctively, my muscles coiled, each breath shallow.

The creature drifts closer, tearing through the mist. Sunlight catches it just long enough for me to see the faint gleam of pale skin, the dark membrane of wings extending from elongated limbs, and the unnatural smoothness of its movement, as if gravity obeys it instead of the other way around.

A snarl builds low in my chest as the scent hits me again, much stronger now, carrying the metallic undertone of something that hunts not for food but for blood itself. My tail stiffens. Instinct surges, demanding I chase, attack, bring it down before it can vanish again, but instinct is not leadership, and every choice I make ripples through the entire pack. Chasing it blindly could result in a trap, and I won't leave my pack vulnerable for the sake of pride.

The creature glides along the ridge, surveying the valley with a beastly predator's patience. Then, as softly as drifting ash, it lifts higher, wings catching an unseen wind, and slides beyond the tree line until it disappears.

The fog settles again, but the dread remains. I turn back toward the heart of Blackwater Pack lands. The valley may be quiet now, but the silence is different. Something unnatural has marked our territory, and it is only a matter of time before it returns–bolder, hungrier, and not alone.

I move along the riverbank, straining for any sign of movement. The morning chill clings to my fur and bites at my paws. The scent of the Nightborn, as scouts and farmers have called them, hangs faintly in the air, a whisper of iron and rot, just enough to keep my focus braided like a tight chain. My instincts bristle; even the forest seems to lean away from their presence, shadows thickening unnaturally among the trees.

A tree ahead catches my attention. Its bark is shredded, deep gashes gouged as if a clawed hand, paw, or perhaps something in between, ripped through with great force. The grooves are long, jagged, and impossibly high off the ground for any wolf. I press closer, my nose twitching, tasting the lingering copper tang, and the hairs along my spine rise. Something has been here. Something stronger, faster, and more clever than any predator I have faced in my lifetime.

I follow the signs further upriver. My paws skim across frozen stones, claws scoring shallow tracks in the icy mud. Fur floats along branches and drifts in the shallow pools of the river, disturbed and tangled where the Nightborn have struck. Every strand is familiar: sheep, wolves, even bears, but marred with dark stains where blood has pooled and dried on hides. These are wounds inflicted in ways no natural predator would use.

I gnash my teeth as a low growl rumbles in my chest. The forest has become a hunting ground for a creature that is neither beast nor human but something far worse, a predator that stalks with intelligence and cruelty, relishing fear as much as blood.

The scouts' whispers echo in my memory, hushed voices trembling as they spoke of glimpses along the tree line–shadows with wings, pale faces reflected in moonlight, eyes red as the blood moon. I remember the first report, the one that made me shift immediately and strike out along the borders. Every tale has been confirmed in the aftermath: missing livestock, torn earth, shredded trees, and yet, they are always just out of reach. The Nightborn are always a step ahead of me, leaving only signs of their passage.

The Nightborn are cunning, but so am I. I have led my pack through harsh winters, defended against rival Alphas, and hunted more dangerous prey than shadows with wings. These valleys are mine. The river, the woods, the frost-bitten ridges, all belong to Blackwater Pack. Whoever, or whatever, these beasts are, they can't be allowed to continue their reign of terror.

Eventually, I reach the edge of the valley, the familiar walls of my castle rising ahead, but relief doesn't fully reach me. The valley is not safe yet; the threat is still out there, hidden in shadows of the night sky, but home calls, and duty demands my hasty return.

Towers and ramparts stand tall, etched against the pale light of dawn, a steadfast reminder of the lands I protect. I move toward the gate and enter the castle. A servant greets me with a change of clothes, so I shift, dress, and then follow the familiar corridors until I reach my bedroom door.

I close the door behind me and strip out of the temporary outfit

I've just put on, dressing in royal garments: the heavy black cloak that marks my authority, black trousers, and the silver tunic with the sigil of Blackwater Pack on the lapel.

The council chamber is quiet when I enter, though scouts and lieutenants are seated, ready to listen, their eyes filled with curiosity. I take my place at the head of the table. Reports are already laid out: sightings, missing livestock, hunter accounts, and the scattered traces left by the Nightborn. I sweep my eyes over each document, memorizing every detail and mapping the patterns.

I lean forward, resting my hands on the edge of the table, and look to Mason, then to the council of warriors, scouts, and elders. "I saw one," I begin, my tone calm but carrying authority. "Above the river, drifting along the ridges. Its wings were long and narrow, its body humanoid but stretched unnaturally long and thin. It observed me but didn't strike."

A murmur rushes through the room, but I raise a hand to demand silence. "It vanished as the sun rose—with no attack, no engagement. That might be a clue as to how their dark magic works. These creatures are not mindless predators. They understand fear and control, seeking blood. Their approach is calculated. They leave evidence of their passage, enough to mark territory, enough to show us they are here, and they know we can track them."

Mason leans forward. "It sounds like they can only attack at night."

"Exactly," I reply. "They hunt livestock, creatures of the forest, and even shifters, but only under cover of darkness."

I let the words settle, giving everyone in the room a moment to take them in before I continue. "We will not underestimate them. We will prepare. Scouts, double-check boundaries. Hunters, patrol with caution. Every warrior must be made aware of the signs that they are nearby, and we will learn from their patterns, the traces they leave, and from every interaction."

The council absorbs the gravity of the report, each member processing the information in their own way. Several nod. A few take notes. Hushed whispers pass between pairs.

"Stay vigilant. Track everything: every scent, every mark, every shadow. The Nightborn are out there, but we won't be caught off guard." I look at each face and wait for acknowledgment, my gaze unwavering.

Outside, the sun climbs higher, burning away the last wisps of darkness. In the clearing light, the Nightborn are gone, but their warnings linger, and I vow that when they return, we will be ready.

4

FRIENDS

I wake slowly, the cold gnawing at my fur. My body shivers despite the warmth of the fire crackling somewhere nearby, and my muscles are stiff and sore from the night's ordeal. The memory of the bats still lingers, their claws, their shrieks, and the sheer terror pressing down on me sends a shudder running through me. I lift my head and strain my eyes against the dim light, sinking into the soft blanket wrapped around me.

I realize I'm not alone. Several people are in the room with me. The cabin smells of herbs and smoke from the fire burning low in the hearth. Shelves sag under jars of powders, dried plants hang from the ceiling beams, and scattered vials and tubes catch the flickering light. A mortar and pestle sit on the table, flecked with green paste, and worn tomes are stacked on the table. Despite the clutter, the space feels purposeful, like a place that was built to prepare for danger and survive it.

A tall man steps toward me, others following. I sit up slightly and look up at him. He dominates the space above me without effort. He's broad-shouldered, muscular, and his presence is almost overwhelmingly authoritative. "You're safe here. I carried you over my back, and Willow healed your wounds."

I nod in thanks, my eyes flickering to a woman standing over his shoulder. She must be Willow. A quick count tells me there are seven of them at all. I tremble at the memories of claws, wings, and fangs, but gratitude seeps in. These rogues saved me.

The woman he alluded to, a beautiful redhead with sapphire eyes, steps forward. "I'm Willow. You should shift so we can speak," she says softly. "You can recover fully in your human form with a little rest. We have clothes you can wear." She motions to a doorway.

I hadn't even realized I was still in my wolf form until now, but I hesitate. Every instinct screams to be cautious. Every muscle tightens against the thought of exposure, but I'm drawn to the friendliness of the group, and I know they mean me no harm. With a nod, I climb from the bed. Willow moves to a door and pushes it open to reveal a small, private room. The floor is cold beneath my paws. Once inside, the shift is quick. Fur recedes, bones reshape, and my mind spins with dizziness and raw relief. Finally, I stand on two legs, still shaking and feeling vulnerable.

A bench is covered with a blouse, trousers, underclothes, a belt, thick wool socks, and a cloak. I dress quickly, tugging the cloak tight around my shoulders, feeling oddly comforted.

Returning to the main room, I find them staring at me. They're not leering or judging but watching curiously. They all give me their attention, yet none overstep.

Willow takes my hand and leads me back to the bed, helping me in and covering me with the blanket. "You should rest now." She pats the blanket and offers a reassuring smile.

The tall, dark, well-built man who carried me here steps forward again. "I'm Havelock." His voice is low. "I make sure no one gets away with hurting the innocent or my friends." He exudes dominance, yet there's something reassuring in it. I can tell he's a protector, not a tyrant.

A man with tousled blond hair falling just above his shoulders and sharp cheekbones steps forward, a grin tugging at his lips. He's lean and quick, and there's a playful glint in his gaze that hints at mischief and cleverness. "I'm Seamus," he says. "I'm an expert tracker and scout. I read the land, follow trails, and find what others can't."

Another of them steps closer, rising to his full height. A dark mohawk runs perfectly down the center of his head, and a large beast tooth from some fierce creature, jagged and worn, hangs from a leather cord around his neck. "They call me Ian." His voice is calm and certain. "I've never lost a battle."

A woman with caramel-colored skin and tightly coiled, curly blonde hair lifts a hand. Her eyes are the color of honey, warm and kind, and she wears a flowing green dress that moves easily with her. "I'm Ivy." A playful smirk tugs at her lips. "Stealth is my game. I can move unseen through towns, forests, shadows, wherever danger hides." She winks, and I feel a twinge of amusement.

A mysterious woman hangs back, near the hearth. Tall and slender, her ebony skin glows in the firelight. A long purple braid drapes over her shoulder, swaying as she moves. It takes her a moment to finally say, "I'm Lark. I sense things others don't. I know when magic stirs and when unnatural forces are near." Her voice is quiet but electric.

The final man rises from where he has been leaning against the wall, tall and broad, with curly auburn hair that falls just past his shoulders and ocean blue-green eyes. His features are strong and rugged, and a faint scar runs along his jawline, hinting at battles fought. "I'm Mac. I excel at scouting, clearing enemies and protecting my allies. We are all exiles from Moonfang Pack, cast out many years ago by Luna Selvara for crimes—real, framed, or imagined, but don't think that makes us weak. Our cohesion, our purpose, and the way we watch out for each other is what keeps us alive."

I nod in understanding. I hope I can keep all of their names straight. "You saved me," I say. "I owe you my life."

Lark tilts her head slightly, her purple braid falling down her back. Her voice is musical, but there's an edge of curiosity. "You don't owe us anything," she says. "Except maybe your name and perhaps your story."

"I'm Xamara, the sole heir of the late Alpha of the Moonfang Pack. Selvara is my stepmother, but I don't agree with the way she runs the kingdom. I was in the midst of my first shift when those creatures appeared out of nowhere, hunting me relentlessly. I got lost in these woods, and they wouldn't let me go."

The rogues exchange glances, subtle nods passing between them, like gears turning silently in their heads. Maybe they're communicating through the mind-link, but I don't think so. I don't think they need it.

Havelock tilts his head. "Moonfang royalty, huh? That explains why they went after you. Blood like yours doesn't go unnoticed by the Nightborn."

I frown. "Nightborn?"

"Yes, the Nightborn," Lark says softly, stepping forward, her gaze dark and penetrating. "Creatures that shouldn't exist. They hunt wolves, but they're not wolves themselves. Not entirely. They're not completely bats either."

"That's right," Seamus adds. "You weren't imagining their strength or their cunning either. They're fast and coordinated like nothing natural should be."

He glances at Mac, who crosses his arms. "They need wolf blood to feed whatever dark magic fuels them. That's why they kept coming after you. You are the last of the blood heirs to your throne. That makes your blood powerful and special to the Nightborn."

"They... they feed on wolves?" I whisper, horrified. "Like ritualistic hunting?"

Willow sits next to me on the bed. "It's worse than that. They don't just feed–they consume blood. It's what strengthens the magic. They grow more dangerous every time they feed, and they're not mindless. Someone, or something, is directing them."

"Your royal blood is exactly what they want," Ivy adds. "You have a target on your back with that white coat. You need to understand. You're not just prey. You're their favorite prey. But you're not alone." Her eyes sweep the group. "We'll protect you."

I take a deep breath, letting their words sink in. *Wolf blood. Dark magic. Nightborn.* The horrifying pieces click together, and my heart races, but beneath it all, a stubborn spark ignites. I might be hunted, but I will *not* cower.

"They can try," I say. "But they won't take me without a fight."

Seamus leans forward slightly, a grin tugging at the corner of his mouth. "That's the spirit."

Willow pats my shoulder. "For now, rest. Gather your strength."

I nod, letting myself sink back into the pillow, and as my eyelids grow heavy, I realize something vital: this house, these rogues–they are no longer strangers. They are my allies, my shields, and my chance to fight back. I want to go home to Moonfang Pack, but I can't yet. If I leave now, those creatures will follow me, and I refuse to put my entire pack in danger. These seven rogues, exiles, warriors, and champions, are the first line of defense between me and the darkness that hunts my blood. They don't have to help me, but they've chosen to. Why, I don't know, but I'm eternally grateful for it.

I WAKE AGAIN HOURS LATER, WARM AND RESTED. MY WOUNDS ARE completely healed, and my mind is clear.

Only one person is in the room with me now. Willow, the beautiful copper-headed healer, sits at the hearth, grinding something in a small wooden bowl while softly humming. When she sees that I'm sitting up, her face brightens.

"Well, look at you," she says. "There's color in your cheeks."

I stretch my arms. "Where is everyone?"

"Out and about." She dusts her hands off as she stands. "They have chores. They've got their own houses scattered around our little clearing, but we gather here when we need to. Speaking of which..." She tilts her head, smiling. "Would you like a tour?"

Part of me wants to crawl back beneath the covers and hide from the world, but another part wants to learn, explore, and see who these people truly are and how they live. "Yes, thank you," I say. "I'd love that."

Willow smiles. "Come on, then." She hands me a pair of boots, and I slip them on.

Outside, the cold air bites my cheeks, but the sky glows gold and pink with the approaching dusk. Snow crunches under our soles, but the clearing is peaceful and so different from last night's terror.

We walk to the nearest house, a structure carved into the hillside. "That's Seamus's den," Willow says.

Through the window, I see Seamus bent over a desk cluttered with maps. He's marking something, his lips moving as he mutters to himself. When he glances up and spots us, he gives a lazy salute before returning to his work.

"He's always scouting the safest hunting routes," Willow murmurs. "He knows these woods better than anyone."

Next is a stone-and-timber home, built neat and methodically. Inside, Ian sharpens a blade, his expression focused and unbothered by the sparks that flick off the whetstone. His mohawk is impressively tall and straight, and from out here, he looks dangerous.

"He'll pretend he doesn't care if you're alive," Willow whispers. "But he truly has the biggest heart."

We move on to Ivy's home, which smells like sage, rosemary, and other herbs. The door is open, and when we peek inside, we find her drying deer jerky. She catches my eye and winks before returning to her work.

Lark's house is brightly lit with violet hued candles, and we hear her chanting to the Moon Goddess through the open windows.

Havelock's cabin sits next to Lark's house, and it's the largest of them all. He's chopping firewood in the yard, stopping only to bow slightly as we walk by.

Mac's house is last. He's stirring something in a large pot over the fire, the rich, savory, mouthwatering scent drifting out.

"Dinner?" Willow calls.

"Almost," he replies without looking up. "I hope you're hungry."

My stomach growls at the smell alone.

Willow laughs softly. "Come on. We all eat together."

In the middle of the clearing, a long wooden table has been set up beside a roaring fire, flames leaping into the darkening sky. The snow around it has been melted, leaving space for chairs and benches. We gather around. Plates are passed. Jokes fly. The evening is filled with friendship and belonging.

I sit between Willow and Seamus, a steaming bowl placed in front of me. The first bite of savory stew melts on my tongue—rich, meaty, comforting.

Mac looks at me from across the table. "You're one of us now," he says simply.

"Thank you," I say. "That means more to me than you could imagine."

The sky darkens rapidly, stars pricking the ebony blanket, and the cold sharpens despite the crackling fire. The laughter and chatter around the table slow, voices lowering, glances moving toward the sky.

Seamus leans back in his chair, his eyes scanning the horizon. "Night's coming," he says quietly. "That's when they move."

Havelock's eyes meet mine. "The Nightborn only hunt in darkness."

Everyone finishes their food, the firelight dancing across their faces. One by one, they rise, heading toward their cabins—for cover. Willow looks at me and smiles. "You can stay in my cabin tonight."

I'm still terrified of the Nightborn, but as I follow Willow, I feel a bond forming with my new friends. I'm safe as long as I'm with them.

5

———

PUPPETS

The fire throws jagged shadows over the clearing, turning the snow around us orange and gold. I sit on a fallen log, mug full of whiskey in hand. Mason sits to my right, scanning the tree line. Across from me, Lorna, my chief alchemist, looks over her notes, muttering under her breath.

"They're certainly clever," she says without looking up. "The ones you saw yesterday at dawn. They move like nothing I've catalogued. They seem to be part bat, part human, with wings that seem too large for the rest of their anatomy."

My Beta, Mason, leans forward. "The real question is, if we can't track them, how do we fight them? How do we defend the pack against huge winged beasts?"

Our healer, Helena, shakes her head. "We don't even know what they are yet. There's no telling if silver will harm them or if the traditional wards–holy symbols, fire, or sunlight–will do anything to slow them down."

"I believe you may be on to something there," I say. "Yesterday morning, as the sun rose higher, the one above me seemed to disappear."

A crack in the underbrush makes us all tense for a moment until we sense two scouts. They stumble into the firelight, one of them carrying something bulky in his arms.

"Alpha," he begins, "we found something you should see."

They drop it, and I rise, stepping forward.

A sheep lies in the snow, its veins empty, as though it's been drained of blood. And yet, there are no marks on the flesh and nothing to explain the absence of blood.

"Tell me exactly what you saw," I demand.

"We found it near the north clearing near the river," the scout says. "No tracks. No claw marks. No bites. No sign of disturbance in the rest of the herd."

Helena whispers, "Blood drained with no wounds is ritualistic. Sorcery."

Lorna nods. "This isn't natural. Dark magic surrounds the Gleabhain River. Perhaps this is vampirism."

I swallow the rising lump in my throat, letting my eyes drift to the sky. The Nightborn are out there. They're taunting us.

Through the mind-link, I give a directive. *"Everyone who isn't a warrior, head home for the night. Make sure the doors are secure, and stay inside until dawn unless otherwise summoned. If you are a healer, please be ready in the mind-link. We might need you tonight."*

I look at the scouts. "You must stick together. Watch over the herds, the shepherds, and the entire pack. Keep alert, and don't leave your post."

Then, I turn to my Beta and the warriors who have gathered nearby. "You'll go with me. We're going into the Gleabhain River Valley to track the Nightborn."

Every detail of the sheep, from the drained veins, to the untouched flesh, and the absence of marks, turns my heart to ice.

"Prepare yourselves," I say. "We run in patrols of five. No one strays, and no one lags. Keep your senses sharp, trust your instincts, and watch for anything unnatural."

I glance at my warriors. Each one is taut with readiness. I feel their energy, their loyalty, their courage, and I feed it with my own confidence. "Every claw mark, every clue, every detail points toward the Nightborn. We will track them. We will kill them, and we will find whoever orchestrated these attacks. We will end whoever is hiding behind their shadowed wings, teaching terror."

I shift, fur bursting from my skin, claws extending, senses sharpening until every sound, smell, and vibration is magnified. The warriors around me follow, shifting in unison. Their bodies are sleek and powerful, their muscles ready for the hunt.

The valley awaits, dark and endless, snow muffling our movements. I lead the patrol. My senses strain for sound, smell, and movement. Every snapped twig, every rustle of branches, every metallic tang of blood sends my pulse racing. My mind calculates, anticipates, and hunts.

Powdered snow bursts beneath our paws as we move through the trees. *"Spread out,"* I order through the mind-link.

Mason takes the left flank, Simeon fans right, and I take the center with two of our fastest wolves. Just as we change formation, a shadow drifts overhead. I snap my head up. Something dives above the treetops, too fast to track, like the shadow of a cloud brushing the moonlight. The snow beneath us has been disturbed. Twisted prints and broken branches mark where something landed or moved too quickly to see. I catch the sharp tang of blood on the wind, the faintest scent of wet fur, and the brush of wings passing just out of reach. The Nightborn are here.

Mason growls. *"Alpha, they're close!"* he shouts through the mind-link.

"Yes," I reply. *"But not close enough. Not yet."*

We move silently with our bodies low, our senses stretched to the edge. The snow is deep in places, slowing some of the younger warriors, but they are disciplined, trained, and unwavering. I rely on them, even as I know the Nightborn will exploit any weakness.

A faint rustle sounds ahead of us. I freeze with my ears twitching. The air smells of blood again, but it's not sheep blood.

"Hold," I command, every muscle tight, my claws flexed. *"Observe. Hold. Prepare for engagement."*

My warriors stiffen behind me, anticipation and tension filling the air.

The forest shivers, a sudden rustle that sets every hair on my back upright. *"Brace yourselves."*

Mason's sharp inhale confirms he's ready. The patrol tightens around me, our muscles wound tight like springs. My mind hums with awareness, every scent and sound amplified.

I realize the Nightborn are no longer just shadows, but they are hunting us, coordinated, almost like they're being guided. But by what? By whom?

A black blur streaks through the trees, slamming into Simeon before he can react. He yelps, snow exploding around him as claws rake across his shoulder.

"Simeon!" I shout. *"Hold your ground!"*

Another bat drops behind Jax. He lunges, his teeth snapping and his claws extended, but the Nightborn twists midair. Its talons graze his flank. Jax spins, growling, but it's gone before he can connect.

I move in closer, feeling the pack's tension radiate through the mind-link. *"Watch the flank. Don't chase blindly,"* I tell them.

The Nightborn descend again, faster this time, flitting between trees. Their wings slice through the air. I leap toward one. My claws extend. My teeth are bared, but it arcs upward. Its wing fold with impossible grace, and it slams into Mason instead. He winces sharply, stumbling, his claws scraping the ground. He forces himself upright, but I can see the strike left a deep cut across his side.

"Alpha, there are too many, and they're too coordinated!" he hisses. I hear the strain in his voice. He's trembling with both pain and anger.

I growl, snapping my jaw. *"We'll adapt. Watch their movements. Anticipate. Protect each other."*

Another Nightborn dives from above. Zara ducks, but a talon drags along her back, ripping flesh and drawing a sharp cry. Kai lunges after it, but it spins midair. Its talons scrape his flank, leaving him yelping and retreating under a large tree.

These beasts are fast, and either they're smarter than normal predators, or they are being controlled by some dark force. My mind races as I try to track patterns. They test us, probing for weaknesses, dividing us, striking in pairs or trios, but always choreographed, never chaotic.

"Don't break formation. Stay close. Attack together."

A shadow flits low. Wings brush the snow, and Mason yelps again as it slams into him, sending him sprawling. *"I've got you!"* I snap, barreling forward. My claws rake the snow as I shove him out of the way just in time. The Nightborn shrieks, twisting skyward before I can retaliate–a blur against the moonlight.

"Alpha! Behind you!" Mason shouts. I spin just in time to see another shape dive for me. I pivot, extending my claws, snapping my jaws, and air brushes against my fur as talons scrape across my shoulder. Pain burns deep, but it fuels me, adrenaline sharpening my senses. I twist, raking at empty air, trying to land a strike, but it's already gone, replaced by another diving shadow.

"Watch the left! Kai, watch my back!" I yell. The mind-link flares with responses, Zara, Simeon, Jax, Mason, and others all confirming they've heard, all trying to coordinate in the mayhem. The Nightborn whip through the trees like a storm, wings flapping, claws raking, their shrill cries echoing against the snow and ice. Every time one of us lunges, our prey vanishes, and yet another attacks from an angle we didn't anticipate.

Zara yelps as one of the beasts grazes her shoulder, shredding her fur. I growl, circling to intercept its next attempt, but it flips and vanishes among the trees. My patrol is bleeding, frustrated, outmatched in speed and reflex, and I can feel their fear mixing with adrenaline through the mind-link.

We need an edge–something to level the playing field. My mind snaps to Lorna and the others back at Blackwater Pack. My alchemists can bend the elements and conjure storms. A thunderstorm tonight, right here in the Gleabhain Valley, could disrupt these creatures mid-flight.

I fire the thought through the mind-link, precise and urgent: *"Lorna! We need you to start a thunderstorm. Now!"*

Through the mind-link, Lorna's voice reaches me. *"Yes, Alpha Julian."*

Another diver catches Jax off guard, a talon scraping across his flank just as the first flashes of lightning tear across the sky, illuminating the forest in blinding white. Snowflakes scatter, whipped by a sudden wind, and I hear the distant low rumble of thunder. The Nightborn falter, their wings twitching in the sudden turbulence. Their patterns wobble. They're disoriented but not yet defeated.

The wind roars as the thunderstorm takes hold, lightning cracking through the trees in jagged streaks, lighting every shadow and forcing the Nightborn to swerve mid-flight. The creatures' precise, coordinated dives are thrown into chaos.

"Stay tight! Don't let them divide us!" My voice cuts through the storm and into the mind-link. Mason struggles beside me, his fur slick with blood, but instinctively, I feel the pack circling him, protecting him.

Lightning cracks again. The forest is bathed in brief, blinding white, and each time it strikes, the fight twists into something more horrific. I see them clearly now, and these aren't just monsters. They have faces like trapped human souls. Their eyes are filled with pain and fury, as if they're imprisoned in grotesque bodies. Their arms and legs snap into unnatural angles, some still human-like while others are elongated, thin and skeletal. Huge bat wings unfold, thin as parchment, filled with veins glowing with something like fire.

They dive again, wings whipping, claws slashing, but every strike is now weakened by the wind and rain. Their shrieks slice through the night, but the terror remains, gnawing at my gut. I glance at my warriors. Their eyes are revealed in the lightning: terror, disbelief, and adrenaline. None of us have ever seen anything like this. Not in the wild. Not even in our nightmares.

Another bolt brightens the sky even more, and we see dozens of them soaring through the air. The sky is riddled with a writhing, screaming mass of bodies that shouldn't exist. I feel their despair and their rage, like a psychic vibration from something controlling them. They are puppets, and their master is somewhere out there, pulling the strings.

If we are ever going to stop this madness, we must find the puppet master.

6

BLACK MAGIC

JULIAN

The forest is alive with movement as we fight in a tight, disciplined formation, the way we've trained for years. My wolves move and strike in perfect rhythm, three of us holding the front, two pushing from the flanks as Nightborn dive through the trees above us. Their leathery wings beat the air in sharp, jarring bursts, sending dead leaves spiraling across the muddy ground near the Gleabhain River.

We've been fighting for hours, but they never tire. They come in a frenzy, swooping low with their talons bared, their red eyes glowing through the shadows. Every time one dives toward us from the front, another sweeps from behind, forcing us to adjust formation again and again. Still, we hold, slashing up at any creature that dares skim too close, using the trees as both cover and leverage.

The storm Lorna called to distract the Nightborn has turned into an all-consuming force, the sky splitting open as thunder shakes the forest floor. Lightning flickers across the canopy, turning the treetops white and blinding. Rain slams into us hard enough to sting even through my thick pelt, flooding the scents around us and making it almost impossible to track the enemies darting through the branches.

I thought the rain would cause them to retreat, but I was almost instantly proven wrong.

Mere moments after the storm began, the Nightborn surged with it, using the wind to hurl themselves at us from angles we can't anticipate. One swoops down the middle of our formation, scattering two of my wolves as its talons shred bark from a nearby tree.

Another dives straight at me, and I meet it mid-leap, my jaws snapping. It veers off before I can make contact, but the attack breaks our shape, and suddenly, the fight becomes pure pandemonium. They are everywhere and nowhere all at once.

The storm tears through the forest with a violence Lorna rarely unleashes, ripping branches free and sending them crashing around us. My warriors try to regroup, struggling to close ranks in the downpour, but the Nightborn keep cutting between us, forcing them apart one by one. Through the mind-link, I feel their confusion, strain, and desperation. I try to push commands into their minds, but the storm crackles through the bond like static, muffling everything. A lightning strike hits a tree so close that the blast of heat scorches the ground. The trunk collapses between two of my warriors, driving them in opposite directions. The storm is working–just not for us. I can't reach Lorna to tell her to stop, either.

With enough concentration, I finally manage to get a thought through the mind-link. *"Retreat! Scatter! Do what you need to do to get to safety!"* I hate telling them this, but I have no choice. We are outmatched.

Jax and Zara disengage cleanly, sprinting into the underbrush in the direction of the keep, but the others are torn away by the storm's shifting winds or blocked by the creatures clawing through our escape routes. I make one more command through the mind-link, *"Retreat! Now, move!"*

A Nightborn drops directly in front of me, its wings flung wide as it crashes into the mud. I lunge to meet it, but another slams into my side from above, knocking me off balance. The two creatures work together, cutting me off from my remaining wolves and forcing me deeper into the forest. I dig my claws into the snowy ground and throw one off, sinking my teeth into its shoulder before it twists free and takes to the sky. The other sweeps past and lands another blow across my back.

I stagger, reaching out through the mind-link, desperation in my voice. *"Lorna, call the storm off! Hurry!"* I pray to the Moon Goddess that she hears me this time.

There's a pause, then I hear her voice, tense and afraid. *"I tried, Alpha,"* she admits. *"I can't.... It's not mine anymore. I can't control it."*

With a deep breath, I accept my fate. The Nightborn's wings beat the air, keeping it suspended just above the ground as its red eyes lock onto mine. I charge, knowing I have no choice but to face it alone, and the fight that follows tears through the forest in a blur of claws, wings, and blood. It strikes, retreats midair, and twists through the rain with unnatural agility. Every time I leap for its throat, it jerks upward just out of reach, only to dive back down with talons aimed for my spine.

The storm roars around us as we crash together again, and this time I manage to catch its wing in my jaws, dragging it out of the air. We hit the ground hard, sliding across mud and broken branches. The creature thrashes violently, trying to tear itself free, but I clamp down harder, ignoring its claws slashing across my ribs. When it twists just enough to expose its throat, I strike with my claws, and the creature disintegrates beneath me in a burst of ash that scatters instantly in the wind.

I struggle to my feet, bleeding, exhausted, shaking, and for a moment I'm completely still as the realization settles. It took my full strength to kill one on my own

My legs tremble, but I force myself forward, each step sending a deep ache through my ribs and down my flank. The storm thins the further I push toward Abrenna Castle, the worst of it swallowed by the thick forest behind me, but the rain still falls in heavy, relentless sheets that sting against my raw wounds. Blood soaks my fur in dark streaks, warm at first, then chilling as the wind cuts through me.

With every movement, my muscles remind me of how close I came to losing that fight, and the knowledge gnaws at me. If a single

Nightborn fought with that level of strength, what waits behind them? The question sits heavy in the pit of my stomach, sharper than the pain shooting through my body. I keep my ears pricked and my nose low, catching any sound that breaks the rhythm of the storm.

The forest feels wrong, the Nightborn's presence still filling the air, evil vibrating through the trees. They were too coordinated and confident tonight, and there were too many of them. The black magic that controls them took over the storm. This battle feels less like an attack and more like a warning. Something larger is brewing, and my gut tells me it's all connected to the displaced coven in the Montelune Mountains that's been restless since they were forced from their territories. If they've aligned themselves with something powerful enough to summon creatures like this in numbers, then tonight was only the beginning.

The castle walls appear through the thinning rain, tall and dark against the bruised sky, the torches along the battlements glowing like small, stubborn stars. I limp toward the gate, and the guards rush to open it, heads bowing in respect and relief the moment they see me. Their emotions hit me through the mind-link—a wave of worry, awe, and confusion at the state I'm in—but I push past them without slowing.

My paws leave bloody prints on the stone floors as I climb the stairs toward my chambers. By the time I reach the door, the last of my strength drains from my limbs, and I shift back into my human form with a sharp pull that makes my vision blur. The injuries ache deeper now, and the cold sinks straight into my skin. I grab clothes from the foot of my bed and dress quickly, biting down against the sting as fabric drags across torn flesh.

Before I put on my shirt, I reach for Helena through the mind-link and call her to my room. She arrives within a few minutes, knocking once before I tell her to come in. She slips inside, her eyes filling with concern at the sight of my injuries before she crosses the space with a bowl of warm water and herbs she's already prepared.

She cleans the gashes across my ribs and stitches the deepest one along my shoulder. I hold still, my jaw clenched, my eyes fixed on the rain sliding down the window as my mind races through strategies. The patrol rotations, reinforcing the wards, mapping the river paths the Nightborn favored tonight, planning how to strike first if they return in greater numbers.

I reach for my Beta, Mason, through the mind-link, finding him quickly. He answers before I can fully form the question, saying they all made it back, shaken but alive, most with only scratches and gashes that have already begun to heal. Relief hits me hard enough that it steals my breath for a moment, but it doesn't ease the pressure tightening my chest. If the Nightborn meant to wipe us out, they probably could have. Tonight wasn't a full assault; it was a test, and someone very powerful is behind it all.

As Helena finishes binding my last wound, I straighten despite the sharp pull of stitches and let my resolve settle into something solid. Whoever is behind these creatures, a witch or a full coven, perhaps a long forgotten enemy, has drawn blood first, on *my* land. I will not wait for them to strike again. I will hunt them down, tear apart their alliances, and end whatever is raising unrest in Vaeloria and Hexeton before it reaches my gates. No matter how cunning, no matter how deadly, no matter how deep into the dark I have to go, I will find the source of the Nightborn and crush it before it destroys everything I am sworn to protect.

I don't waste time once Helena finishes. I pull my shirt on, ignoring the sting of the wounds beneath it. My body screams for rest, but the pressure, fear, strategy, and fury all tangle together, leaving no room for weakness. Through the mind-link, I summon Lorna to the council chamber, as well as Mason, Kai, Zara, Jax, and Simeon. They are my most loyal warriors.

I stride down the hall, and by the time I push open the doors to the war room, the others are already gathered. Mason stands at the head of the table, his arms crossed, his mouth pursed in concentration. Lorna paces near the hearth, her hands restless, the storm outside still ignoring her power. Kai and Zara speak quietly in the corner while Jax and Simeon stand watch near the windows, their eyes on the storm-wracked sky.

I take the seat at the head of the table, and the room settles instantly.

Mason speaks first. "The storm is being controlled by the enemy."

"Yes, I know. Whoever is controlling those beasts took over the storm. And it seemed to make them stronger. It was a bad idea. I hoped to make it more difficult for them to fly, not make it easier for them to fight."

Lorna's eyebrows knit together. "My storms disrupt magic. They always have. The enemy should've lost control, scattered, and broken apart. I don't know who is playing with the black magic it takes to steal a conjured storm, but they are a very powerful force, Alpha."

"The storm made them move faster," Zara adds. "They flew harder. Hit harder."

Kai leans forward on the table. "I saw one dive straight through a lightning strike and come out faster."

"That shouldn't be possible," Lorna whispers, shaking her head.

I meet her eyes. "Someone formidable was feeding them power. Bolstering them. Using *your* storm as a conduit."

"The displaced coven," Mason says. "It has to be."

"I think you're right," I agree. "Desperation mixed with ambition."

Jax glances at the bandages under my shirt. "They pushed too far."

"We all made it back alive, thank the Moon Goddess," I say. "We rest tonight, tend our wounds, and then, at sunrise, we track their movements back to their lair. They have to seek shelter somewhere, don't they? We track them all the way to the source."

Zara looks at me. "And when we find them?"

I stare out the window at the raging storm, the choreography of something dark in the distance. "We end this."

Everyone in the room nods in grim agreement. Tonight has left its mark, and even as most of Blackwater Pack sleeps, I'm reminded that power is never given. Power is seized, and those who hesitate pay the price. I am their Alpha, their protector, and the choices I make in the dark will echo long after this bloody night has passed.

7

WITCH HUNT

We move through the forest in wolf form, daylight cutting through the trees. It's not the best time to hunt Nightborn, but the rogues insist we follow the trail now because they leave traces behind whatever darkness hides.

I fall into step beside Seamus, his nose glued to the snow, body low and fluid, his pale blond fur catching the light. He glances at me, ears flicking, and mutters through the mind-link, *"It would be easier if it weren't winter."* Because of my royal blood, I'm able to mind-link with anyone who used to be a part of my pack—even these rogues who have essentially formed their own pack, and their own mind-link, over the years.

Havelock pads behind us, his massive black paws crunching through the snow, his dark fur blending into the shadows, his eyes scanning the treetops. Every few steps, he stops, sniffing the air like he can swallow the forest whole. *"They came this way. I smell fresh blood."*

Ivy flits along the edges, her honey-caramel fur keeping her warm against the cold. Her tail brushes the ground as she darts ahead and then circles back. She pauses on a ridge with her nose twitching. *"The storm last night has washed most of the scent and blood from the snow, but I think they went this way."* Her tone is playfully mischievous, even in wolf form, and I almost forget we're hunting death itself.

Lark's lavender coat blends with the shadows of the winter-dusted pines. She moves with her ears forward and her muzzle lifted. *"That storm was brought here by magic,"* she whispers through the mind-link. *"It wasn't natural. Whoever sent the Nightborn sent that storm. I can feel the magic pulling east."*

Mac exhales beside me, his nostrils flaring. *"The witches live in the mountains to the east. I bet the trail leads us straight to them."*

When we reach the riverbank, our paws sink into the snow and ice along the edge. The ground is torn, branches snapped, and tufts of fur are scattered across the frozen earth. Dark stains of blood streak the snow, evidence of a recent battle.

Pausing, I take a deep breath, my ears swiveling to catch every scent. *"Which packs are nearby?"* I ask, looking at the rogues as they fan out along the bank, sniffing and scanning.

Seamus lifts his head. *"The closest territory? Blackwater Pack. It could've been Blackwater that the Nightborn hit. That might explain why the trail leads here."*

"It doesn't matter. Alpha Julian likely didn't finish them off, and we're the ones following them now." Havelock spits the Alpha's name out like a curse. I don't know the man, but it seems the rogues aren't so fond of him.

"We must be cautious," Lark warns. *"Whoever controls them will soon notice us. Royal blood is a meal they can't ignore."*

The snow crunches under our paws as we follow the clues on the riverbank. More torn branches, shredded bark, and frozen pawprints mark a large area where the battle took place. The rogues and I fan out, instincts honed, circling, sniffing, and scanning. Even Willow's small form moves quickly, yet silently, noting the marks of battle, her nose twitching as if she's memorizing every scent.

I pause, catching all seven rogues in motion around me, each so distinct even in wolf form: Havelock the immovable shield, Seamus the cunning scout, Ivy the silent striker, Lark with the unnatural sixth sense, Mac the calculated hunter, Ian the manic strategist, and Willow the quiet, deadly healer. They aren't just exiles that my stepmother cast out. They've already become friends to me, and they've chosen to fight to keep me safe. Loyalty and respect bloom in my chest. Nightborn or witch, predator or puppet-master, we'll meet them head-on, together.

By mid-afternoon, the scent of the Nightborn grows thick, pungent, impossible to ignore. It tangles with the crisp mountain air, dragging hints of iron-tinged blood toward us.

Seamus moves ahead, low to the ground, tail whipping as he reads every scent, and every torn patch of moss. *"We're close. Very close,"* he mutters.

Havelock's massive shoulder brushes my side when he lopes up beside me. *"Good. I'm glad they're close. Finally, we're not chasing ghosts."* The tension in him coils, ready to spring at the first sign of danger. I see it in his eyes.

"I love it when whatever we are hunting actually fights back," Ivy says, her tail high and her ears forward as she darts through the under-brush. *"It keeps us sharp."* She weaves around a tree and then crouches low, her nose twitching.

Lark drifts near the ridge with her ears pricked. She lifts her eyes to the ridges above. *"There are the caves,"* she says. *"They've made their lair high above us. Magic radiates from these stones."*

The sun dips low behind the mountains. Shadows stretch long across the crags. Out of nowhere, the first beat of wings cuts through the quiet. A Nightborn bursts from a cave mouth. Its leathery wings slice through the air while its red eyes are fixed on us. Its scream is not animalistic, not human, but a hollow, echoing shriek that rattles my bones.

"Stick together! Defensive formation!" Havelock commands as he swings wide, his fangs bared, fur bristling.

I whirl toward the first creature. My teeth snap in its direction. It dives low at me with its claws aimed for my flank, but I leap, dodging just in time. Another Nightborn twists from the shadows and lunges directly at me. My muscles scream as I strike, my fangs ripping through its wing, but there's another already on my side.

Maybe I shouldn't be here. I would hate for any of the rogues to get hurt defending me.

"I've got you, Xamara!" Ivy calls as she lunges at a Nightborn about to strike me, forcing it to twist midair.

Willow is everywhere at once, a blur of copper fur, circling and distracting, pulling attackers away from me. *"They'll have to do better than this!"* she yells, spinning into a swipe that clips a creature's chest.

Havelock catches another in his jaws, swinging it into the rock wall with bone-shattering force. Lark moves like a spirit through the battle. Every creature that draws near her falters, their wings flailing as if she bends reality slightly around us. *"Focus,"* she whispers. *"Use the power of the moon."*

A new scent hits us as a pack of coal-black wolves, their fur so dark it almost absorbs the fading light, emerges, led by a wolf I assume to be their Alpha. He towers over everyone else, his glowing amber eyes sweeping the battlefield, and with a commanding snarl, the Nightborn hesitate, retreating to the sky, unsure. The Alpha's presence seems to change the momentum of the skirmish.

When the Nightborn hit us again, the black wolves launch into the fray. Fangs snap and bodies strike with precision. The rogues coordinate instinctively, like they always do. Mac and Havelock take the front, Seamus and Ivy circle, while Lark and Willow provide cover for me. Every Nightborn they strike turns to ash on contact, but the creatures are relentless. Their claws slash. Their fangs snap, and their dark wings whip up snow and stone.

One Nightborn breaks through toward me, its red eyes blazing. I dive, rolling as claws tear through my side. Pain flares white-hot. Just as it lunges again, the black Alpha intercepts. His jaws clamp around its torso, and he drags it into the snow.

The Nightborn begin to retreat. Many crumble into ash. Others take to the skies, flapping into darkness. The forest is quieter now, with blood-soaked patches of earth and tufts of fur scattered across the ridge.

Panting, I sink into the snow, my muscles trembling. The rogues gather around protectively. We're all exhausted but alive.

Ivy steps beside me, breathing hard. *"Not bad for your first real attack."*

Havelock adds. *"You held your own."*

"Not bad at all. You might even survive the next round," Seamus teases, flopping onto the ground next to me.

Lark's lavender tail swishes. *"They were definitely after you, Xamara. Yours is the blood they seek."*

I scan the ridge with my heart pounding in my chest and spot the coal-black warriors still stationed behind us. Their fur reflects the silver moonlight. Every stance is alert, every muscle ready for action. At their center, the Alpha looms, massive and unyielding, and his eyes are fixed on the craggy mouths of the caves.

Another round of Nightborn burst from the cave mouths with a feral screech. Somehow they seem even larger, more monstrous, than before as they plunge toward us. The rogues tighten around me, baring their teeth and flicking their tails with their ears forward.

Willow moves close, just behind me, her small form deceptively strong. She darts forward when a Nightborn sweeps low. Her teeth sink into its wing. *"Xamara, stay near me!"* she hisses through the mind-link.

One creature claws across my flank, and I yelp, spinning into Ivy's intercept. The golden rogue snaps at the Nightborn, forcing it off balance just enough for Willow to land a clean bite.

Havelock and Mac take the front line together, a wall of muscle and calculated power. I watch Havelock swing a creature toward Mac. The other rogue clamps down and shakes it as if it were a toy. I can't help the glimmer of awe that runs through me. They move as one, knowing exactly where the others will be, and the coal-black wolves fight on the perimeter with deadly grace.

A silver flash of fur fills my peripheral vision, and Ian says through the mind-link, *"Watch the right flank."* Instantly, Seamus and Ivy adjust their positions.

Two of the creatures barrel toward me, faster than before. Claws rake through my side, tearing muscle and fur, and I stumble back, sliding on the ice-crusted ground. Pain explodes along my ribs, my vision blurring at the edges, and I realize, with a jolt, that I am completely cornered. One Nightborn dives on my left. Fangs snap inches from my throat; the other sweeps from the right, its claws scraping against my neck.

I taste blood in my mouth, and my mind screams for me to run, to fight, but there's no room to even move, no leverage, only terror and the searing pain of being torn apart.

A shadow seems to descend from the sky. Lifting my eyes, I see the black Alpha crashing in. His teeth clamp down on one Nightborn, and he shakes it with such force that it splinters the air with a shriek, while his massive paws slam another into the rocky ridge. A third collapses under his jaws, the sound of cracking bone echoing across the mountainside. The two on top of me hesitate for a fraction too long, and I seize the moment, rolling away.

The remaining Nightborn retreat, shrieking, their wings beating a violent rhythm against the wind. Their red eyes flare with rage, but the Alpha's presence, along with the rest of his pack, forces them back toward the caves.

Willow is beside me, her fur bristling and her teeth still bared. *"You're okay,"* she says softly through the mind-link. *"You're alive, and you're going to be fine."*

I look at the sky and see one injured Nightborn struggling to fly away, its wing mangled, trailing sparks of dark magic. The rogues tighten around me, all eyes on the injured, retreating creature. Without hesitation, we follow, keeping our distance. Our noses and instincts track every falter in its flight. It limps toward the largest cave mouth, disappearing into shadows far deeper than I imagined.

On the perimeter of the cave, the heat of hundreds of them radiates from inside, their presence a pulsing, unnatural mass of movement. My stomach twists with fear and fascination. Hundreds of Nightborn are bound to the coven that controls them.

The rogues exchange glances. Havelock's dark muzzle tilts toward the trail down the mountain. *"We've seen enough for today. We must regroup, heal, and plan."*

Ivy pads beside me and nudges my side. *"We'll get them next time. We'll be ready."*

From the ridge above, I see the Alpha and his pack retreat into the tree line. Even from a distance, questions swirl through me. Why were they here? Why did they intervene, and what do they want from the Nightborn? I can't shake the unease beneath my fascination.

By the time we reach the base of the mountains, the coal-black pack is completely gone. We retreat quietly, tired but alive. I glance at the rogues. There's no doubt in my mind that our path is set. The Nightborn belong to the coven; we've seen it for ourselves. Whatever darkness they serve, whatever magic binds them, we will stand against it together.

8

WHO IS SHE?

The fur along my flank is matted with warm, sticky blood, and every step sends a jolt of pain through the gash in my ribs. The Nightborn's claws cut deep, almost to the bone. I push through the pain anyway. My warriors keep a tight formation around me as we descend the ridge, but none of us speak through the mind-link. The silence isn't comfortable. Failure and shame accompany us on our long retreat.

I replay the fight in my head on repeat. The white wolf, a flash of her pale fur, blood on the snow, and her body pinned between two of the damnable Nightborn.

My gut lurches at the memory. In another second, they would've torn her in half. I don't know why the thought unsettles me so greatly. I don't even know her. Yet, my pulse spikes even now, as if my body recognizes danger in a way my mind hasn't caught up to.

We reach the lower forest, weaving between the charred trunks left from last night's lightning storm. Simeon presses closer, scanning for movement. *"Alpha, did you see the white wolf and her soldiers follow the wounded beast?"* he asks.

"Yes. They pushed their way up to the caves. Dangerous as hell," I

mutter. *"And we should've been right behind them. I backed off. Maybe I shouldn't have."* Though I wanted to stay, I knew my warriors were exhausted, several of them wounded, so we needed to retreat.

"It was clear the Nightborn wanted her, Sir," Mason adds.

I imagine the white wolf with the silver undercoat, the one who fought like she had nothing left to lose. Even wounded, even cornered, she didn't break or beg. She matched my pace, my ferocity; she faced death like an equal, but there's something about her scent. It's familiar, and yet, at the same time, it's threaded with something ancient and volatile that made the Nightborn overcome with hunger.

We push forward. The ache in my side deepens, but I don't dare slow. When the castle walls finally rise through the fog, my warriors sigh in relief. The black stone towers stretch jagged against the snow-blurred sky, flames from the torches dancing along the battlements. My home. My people. My responsibility.

The gates open before us. The guards bow, but their eyes are moving over our injuries. I nod and move on as quickly as I can. Once inside my chambers, I shift. Bones crack back into place with a familiar burn. I pull on clean trousers. Helena doesn't need to be summoned this time. She knocks once. I call out for her to enter, and she stitches me up in silence. Afterward, I put on a dark shirt and look at myself in the mirror. The man looking back at me is barely recognizable, so weighed down with worry over his pack–and the fear that retreating was a mistake.

By the time I reach the war room, most of my warriors are already gathered. A few come in later after visiting other healers. I certainly wasn't the only one wounded in the fray.

Maps and markers scatter across the table like the aftermath of a storm. The moment I stand to speak, all voices cut off. The tension is thick enough to taste.

I step up to the table and scan the maps, hearing every detail my warriors spill without interruption. Simeon gestures to a scorched section of the ridge. "They fought like predators, Sir. The Nightborn didn't seem too interested in attacking anyone but her. Every strike, every screech, it was her they truly wanted."

Mason leans over the table, pointing to scattered markings on the map near the mountain range. "They moved like they'd been trained, coordinated to herd her into the caves, and even then, she didn't stop fighting."

I nod, letting the memories sink in. I saw it with my own eyes, but their retelling sharpens the picture, hones the edges. Why were the Nightborn pulled toward the white wolf? It's as though they shared an unnatural instinct that made them focus on her above all else.

My curiosity about her turns into a raw, unrelenting obsession. It lodges in my chest, pulling my thoughts back to her, no matter how hard I try to focus on strategy. The way her white fur caught the dying light, the determination in her ferocity, the way the Nightborn instinctively went for her... I *need* to know her.

"I don't care what it takes," I say. "We strike back. However many times we have to. The Nightborn are the symptom. The coven, their master, is the disease."

"Then we cut out the disease," Simeon says. "But the coven hasn't shown themselves openly in years. They use creatures and weather as shields. They never step into a fight themselves."

"That's true," I say. "The Nightborn aren't hunting because they're starving and need food. They're being sent. Directed." My gaze drifts to the map, to the caves carved into the ridge. "Whoever commands them wants one thing, and it isn't territory. It's blood."

Mason clears his throat. "If the coven is escalating, Alpha, we need to stack up the outer defenses. We need extra patrols and wards in the lowlands near the river."

"You're right, but I'm afraid that's not enough." I shake my head, the decision settling like an axe slamming into oak. "Defenses won't stop this. We've been patching wounds for too long."

Simeon straightens. "Sir... you're saying—"

"I'm saying we take the fight to the coven. This is war."

A ripple of shock moves through the room. They try to mask it, but the tension sharpens. War isn't new to us, but declaring war is not something we take lightly. Declaring war invites retaliation before dawn. Declaring it puts the castle, the families inside it, the future of our pack, and everyone in the villages at immediate risk. But in this case, we have no choice.

"The Nightborn targeted the white she-wolf for a reason. Something about her blood, her lineage, whoever she is, has made her valuable to the coven, and if they want her, I need to know why they want her."

Mason nods. "Your command?"

"Take a select group. Only the ones who can move fast and think even faster." I gesture toward the northern path on the map. "We track the white wolf and her warriors. We find out where they came from, what they know, and why the coven wants her. She must be brought back alive."

Simeon asks quietly, "And if her warriors resist?"

"We'll have to find a time to take her when they're… distracted," I answer.

The room falls quiet, not in doubt but in a kind of grim acceptance. My warriors exchange looks, silently weighing who among them can handle the task ahead: following the white she-wolf without alerting her, keeping a distance, observing, and separating her from her friends.

Maps and markers sit scattered across the table, but tonight isn't about tactics or battle formations. We discuss routes, possible sightings, and how to shadow her without being seen.

When the last detail lands in place, I clear my throat. "We reconvene at dawn. Rest while you can. Tomorrow we move."

Eventually, the war room empties, and I rub a hand over my ribs, feeling the skin tightening where the wound has already begun to seal. It aches, but the pain is background noise now. The real bruise is somewhere deeper, lodged under my sternum where I keep the truths I don't admit aloud.

I leave the war table behind and head down the corridor. The castle is quiet this late, the air chilled enough to sting the edges of my healing skin.

I reach my chambers and shut the heavy door behind me. In the privacy of the dim firelight, I peel off my shirt and drop it onto the chair by the hearth. My mind feels cavernous tonight, too aware of every thought I've tried to ignore since the ridge.

I lower myself onto the edge of the bed, my elbows braced on my knees. For a moment, I simply breathe, waiting for my mind to settle. It doesn't.

Who is she?

The white she-wolf with blood in her fur and hell in her eyes. The woman the Nightborn swarmed, like starving vampires scenting fresh blood. Why did the Nightborn want her so badly?

And why, in the name of the Moon Goddess, am I still thinking about her?

I drag a hand through my hair, frustration cutting through the exhaustion. There are no answers yet. Only the memory of her white coat, pure as the snow, and the unshakable instinct that she is either a threat or salvation. I don't yet fully understand.

Tomorrow, I'll find her. Not just because the coven wants her, not just because she might hold the key to this war, but because something within me refuses to let her go. Something in me recognizes her, even if I shouldn't.

I lean back on the mattress, the distant howl of the wind threading through the castle stones. Sleep doesn't come easy, but when it does, it brings only one image with it: her.

I run. My paws hit the soft spring grass, each blade bending beneath the wind tugging at my coat, the air filled with her scent. The white she-wolf, brilliantly untouchable, moves ahead, her fur bright against the green, every stride perfect and teasing. Behind her, seven others weave through the meadow, moving with the same rhythm, the same purpose, but it is her I track, her I crave.

She glances back, blue fire in her eyes, and I sense that heat as a dare, a challenge. Chase me if you can, she seems to say, and the air hums with electric flirtation. My muscles coil, my claws dig into the earth, and my heart hammers against my ribs. The meadow stretches wide, wildflowers swaying in the wind, petrichor filling my lungs with each breath, thanks to the recent rain. I surge forward, weaving through her pack, brushing past their coats, but my eyes always stay on her, vibrant white gleaming against emerald green.

We dance through the meadow, our bodies in perfect symmetry. Her movements are taunting, graceful, teasing, always just out of reach. The sun warms the ends of her fur, and I catch the flash of something more than wildness in her gaze. There's a promise and a game that only I seem to understand. I leap, she twists, and the world spins in a riot of color and sound. Every instinct I have screams to keep her close, to protect her, and to never let her out of my sight.

Ahead, the ground tilts, rises, and I sense it before I see it. There's a cliff here with black water coiling beneath the rocks like ink. She doesn't falter. Her eyes lock on mine, and in that moment, I realize she wants me to follow, wants me to see, wants me to reach, and she's not afraid. My chest tightens as I push harder, claws skimming soil, the smell of her intoxicating, pulling me faster than I have ever moved.

Then, in the instant before she should fall, she shifts. Her wolf body dissolves into a woman with long black hair falling in a silk cascade, pale skin that glows in the sun, lips vibrant crimson, and eyes the blue of a sky before a storm. When she tilts her head toward me, it's a silent invitation. I want to catch her, to hold her, to drag her back from the edge of the darkness. I lunge. My paws scrape the earth stretching toward her.

She falls. The cliff claims her, and the black water swallows her beauty and her wildness all at once. I skid to the edge, peering over, my heart broken and jagged, my breath ragged. The roar of the water echoes in my ears, and then I see them. Thousands of huge Nightborn beasts fill the cliff beneath me, their eyes glowing scarlet, their talons scraping against stone. My fur bristles. My teeth snap. My body tenses.

I jerk awake. My chest heaves. I've dug my fingernails into the sheets that are no longer grass. My heart is still racing, and sweat prickles my skin. The ceiling above me reveals nothing.

Her face, that impossible, terrifying beauty, haunts the back of my eyes. Her blue eyes, her black hair, ivory skin, and the ghost of white fur running through the meadow. I don't know her, but I can't stop wanting her.

Who is she?

9

BLACKWATER PACK

Xamara

Sunshine paints the small room in Willow's cabin with a pale gold glow. I stir in my borrowed bed, muscles stiff. Willow is already awake, sitting cross-legged on the floor, her fire-red hair pulled up on top of her head as she tends a small fire. She looks up and gives me a smile. "Good morning." She tosses on one more log before dusting her hands off and turning toward me. "Everyone's gathering outside."

I swing my legs off the bed, stretch, and inhale the crisp winter air drifting in from the slightly open window. My body still stings with the memory of yesterday's battle with the Nightborn, the ash, the rogues fighting as one, but now, surrounded by friends, it feels possible to breathe again.

Outside, the rogues are all coming out of their cabins to greet the morning, gathering in the middle where they eat breakfast. Willow and I get dressed and then go out to join them.

"I'm starving." Havelock yawns, scratching his head. "I think we're almost out of supplies. We need to hunt."

The group murmurs in agreement. Seamus cocks his head. "Elk. I hear them rustling through the trees off in that direction. If we split

55

and circle, we'll catch them before they get too high up the mountains."

With nods all around, we each seek privacy behind the trees and strip to shift. Fur prickles along my spine, claws extend from my fingertips, and within seconds, we are all in wolf form.

We are shadows moving through the frost-bitten forest, each rogue instantly recognizable in his or her distinctive coat. I'm learning to recognize their expressions and facial features, but it has helped knowing each of them is a different color.

The elk come into view, grazing in a meadow dusted with frost. Havelock and Mac move to the front, Seamus and Ivy fan wide, Lark drifts along the ridge, Ian positions for precision, and Willow flits close to me. We close the circle, silent, predatory, and then we surge forward. Snow sprays under pounding paws as adrenaline burns through me.

At first, I help take down as many of the elk as I can. But when a large cow runs through the trees, I tail her. Unable to bring her down by myself, I pause. That's when I realize I've drifted too far. The forest here is quieter, the snow unbroken except for my own tracks and those of the elk, and I can't sense the others anywhere. My ears twitch and my muscles tighten. Something doesn't feel right.

I reach out to the others through the mind-link, *"I must've gone too far. I don't see you, and can't catch a scent."*

"We're over here, Xamara. On the western side of the meadow," Ivy replies. Relief hits me, and I sprint toward them.

A snap of a branch to my left makes me freeze. Two figures appear at the edge of the clearing, silhouetted by the morning sun. Mounted on horses, black and silver symbols gleaming on their armor, they exude lethal authority. Wolves flank them at the tree line, coal black blending with the shadows.

Growling, my fur bristles while my claws dig into the ground. The wolves paw and growl right back, baring their pointy teeth with their eyes locked on me. I am alone, separated from the rogues, and the calm coordination we usually share feels impossibly distant. Every instinct screams to run, to fight, and to survive.

I turn to try to escape, but they surge forward. Instinctively, I whirl around, ready to strike. The black wolves flank me, familiar and fierce, just like the ones we saw last night tearing through the Night-born. They're organized, efficient, and intimidating.

I lunge at the nearest wolf, fangs snapping, claws raking through the snow. It dodges easily, circling, and I twist to strike another, but they keep coming, relentless and coordinated. The soldiers on horse-back ride straight at me, ropes in hand. I leap, trying to bite, slash, push them back, but before I can twist free, a rope lassos my back legs, dragging me down. Another has me by the neck, and then a leather muzzle is clamped around my snout. I bite at it, scraping thick leather with my teeth, and thrash. My claws shred the snow and ice, but I can't break free. With a low chuckle, one of the soldiers tightens the rope around my front legs, pinning them together, while another pulls the one around my hind legs. The ropes bite into my fur. My muscles strain against the binds. Fighting is only making me tired.

The soldiers jerk me toward a waiting carriage. I crash against the wooden side, my teeth gnashing against the muzzle. They slam the door, bolting it behind me. I huff and growl, sliding along the floor, pressing against the walls, but there's nowhere to go. The wolves outside pad around in perfect formation, watching, waiting. I can feel them, their discipline, their readiness, the same order and strength that made the Nightborn retreat last night. Panic presses into me, but instinct flares. I thrash, bite, trying anything to break free until I tire out and have no choice but to still.

The ride is long. I'm jostled over rough roads, the sound of hooves pounding rock. I strain to read the path, trying to catch the scent of the rogues, but it's no use. I must be too far away now to reach them through the mind-link, too. Damnit! If only I had thought of that before we started to move. The smell of pine and frost fades, replaced by damp stone and smoke as we approach a castle.

The carriage stops with a harsh jolt. Before I can get my footing, I'm dragged out, hitting the cold ground. A hand presses against my back, forcing me forward. One of the soldiers crouches slightly, his voice low and sharp. "I'm going to untie the ropes around your legs now. You'll walk with me, or there will be consequences."

With a firm tug, he loosens the ropes around my legs, freeing me. Every instinct screams to fight, but I have no choice. There are too many of them, and I have nowhere to go. I stumble forward on uneven stone as they lead me toward the door. Another soldier removes my muzzle. I growl at him but fight the urge to bite.

Inside the castle, I'm brought to a chamber with heavy oak doors that close behind me with a solid thud. My eyes dart to every corner. The room is small but functional, with bare stone walls and a single window letting in pale light. All I can see are a table, a basin, and a stack of clothes on a chair, but no escape.

One of the warriors shouts outside the door. "Shift and dress."

Again, I have no choice. I close my eyes. Muscles constrict, bones twist, my paws shrink, and my snout retracts. In moments, I am standing on two legs, my human form restored.

I put on a simple tunic, pants, and boots. "I'm dressed," I shout through the door, "and I'd really love to know who the hell kidnapped me and what the fuck is going on!"

The door swings open with a low groan, and the warrior gestures sharply for me to follow. The corridors are wide, cold, and lined with torches. My every nerve is on edge, every sense straining.

The guard doesn't speak. He leads me through a massive doorway into a hall so vast that I struggle to take it all in. Black banners embroidered with silver stretch from the vaulted ceiling, catching the morning light that filters through huge windows.

And then I see him.

Sitting on an elevated throne at the far end, he stares at me. I can't help but notice his strong jaw, high cheekbones, and chocolate brown eyes that seem to pierce right through me. Muscular, he sits with his back ramrod straight, his broad shoulders filling the throne. Black and silver banners surround him, filled with the same intricate symbols etched into the throne. His presence pulls me immediately with a gravity I can't resist. My feet move toward him against my will. He doesn't rise, doesn't speak, but I feel the pull of his power.

"Alpha Julian." The guard's voice echoes off the stone walls.

I take another hesitant step forward, and my chest tightens. The draw is undeniable, magnetic, and instinctual. Something deep inside me hums, resonating with him. This Alpha, this king, this wolf, is different.

He leans forward with his gaze fixed on me. "What is your name?" His voice is calm, much kinder than I expected, particularly given the way I've been treated on our journey here.

I wouldn't be able to keep from answering him, even if I wanted to. "I am Xamara of Moonfang Pack."

Dark orbs roam over my face, as if he's trying to memorize my every detail. "It's nice to meet you, Xamara."

A sarcastic grunt escapes my lips. "I'd like to say the same, but I don't much appreciate how I was treated on the way here."

His eyebrows knit together, and he tips his head to the side. "Whatever do you mean?"

"I mean… I was abducted–bound and muzzled." Despite the intensity of his gaze, I look right into his eyes and fold my arms. "Thrown into a carriage like a sack of refuse. Is that how you treat all of your guests, or is it just my lucky day?"

Somehow, Julian's eyes grow even darker. He turns to the nearest guard. "Gather the men who brought her in. Have them meet me in the war room at once."

The guard nods, moving quickly to obey. The Alpha's focus snaps back to me, letting out a soft sigh, but the tension in his shoulders and the intensity in his eyes remain. "Xamara, I apologize." He shakes his head, finally dropping his eyes from my face. "It was never my intention for you to be treated that way. I thought my orders were clear…."

"Either you're not very good at giving commands, or your soldiers don't obey you. Regardless, it seems that you have a problem here–Alpha." I can't help the snark, despite his sincere apology. If my step-mother gave a command that was disobeyed so blatantly, there wouldn't be anyone left to tell the tale.

He swallows hard, and I can't tell if he's trying to fight the urge to shoot back at me, or if he's just taken off guard by my directness. All he says is, "It will be reconciled."

10

GILDED CAGE

I lead Xamara into the war room. Even after everything she's endured, she walks with her head held high, her shoulders back. Nothing she's been through has broken her spirit.

The members of the guard who brought her in stand stiffly around the table. Most of them fail to look at me. Those who do cannot hold my gaze. The leader of the group rubs a hand across his chin and shuffles his feet.

Offering Xamara the seat next to mine, I sit and take a deep breath. My voice cuts across the table like a whip. "Explain to me exactly what you thought you were doing." The words barely leave my mouth before the anger in my chest flares. "I sent you to bring her back safely. I did *not* send you to abduct her, terrorize her, treat her like she is the enemy, and drag her through the forest." My gaze sweeps the room, hard and unyielding. "What the hell happened?"

Their heads dip even further, murmurs of apology spilling from their lips. Clark, the leader, speaks up. "Alpha, we just wanted to—"

"I don't want excuses. You failed in your duty," I cut in sharply. "You treated a guest of our pack as if she were an enemy. That will not happen again!" I slam my fist down on the table, shaking the entire room. Everyone jumps–except for Xamara.

There's a pause, and then they nod, shame clear in their eyes. "I need time to consider the consequences, but believe me, they are forthcoming. Now, get the fuck out of my sight."

Clark's mouth moves again, but he does not speak, which is one of the few smart decisions he's made today. They file out, leaving Xamara and me alone. There's a gravity to her presence that refuses to be ignored, and I feel it tug at me like nothing I've ever felt before. I push the feeling down, a desire I know I can't indulge. "Are you certain you weren't harmed?" My voice is much gentler now. I turn to her, trying to read her expression.

She meets my eyes. "I'm fine, thank you. When are you going to tell me why I'm here?"

"You're here so we can talk about what happened in the mountains last night," I say. "With the Nightborn."

Her gaze shifts to the wall across from us as she sighs. "They were targeting me, and I don't know why."

I nod. "I believe they're controlled by the coven. That would explain their location, coordination, and ruthlessness."

Xamara looks at me, studying my face for a moment. Trust is earned, after all. Finally, she says, "Yes. They're not just random predators. Someone is sending them to torture and kill members of my pack. We traced their movements and noted patterns. Their attacks are organized and strategic."

"You've faced them directly," I say. "And you're still standing. Few could survive what you endured."

"I've been through worse," she says quietly, but the pain behind it is unmistakable. She doesn't elaborate, doesn't ask for reassurance, and doesn't invite pity. There's a resilience there I can't ignore.

"How did you come to be friends with your soldiers? Were you cast out by your pack?"

"I was in the middle of my first shift when the Nightborn attacked me the first time and drove me onto your territory. Several members of my pack were slaughtered. My friends are rogues, but they helped me."

I tip my head to the side, trying to understand. Those skilled fighters were all rogues? "You were on Moonfang territory when the beasts attacked you the first time?"

"That's right," she says.

I shift closer to her. "And has Moonfang dealt with those creatures before? Had you seen them before?"

With a shrug, she says, "I had never seen such evil creatures in all my life."

"You're remarkably candid," I say. "Most people would try to hide their knowledge considering what my guards just put you through. I respect that, but I also sense you're holding back. What is it that you're not telling me?"

A sarcastic chuckle escapes those perfect red lips. "Of course, I haven't told you everything. You're a stranger who just kidnapped me."

Her answer only sharpens the questions in my mind. Why has she drawn the Nightborn's attention so fiercely? Why is she able to withstand them in ways even my warriors would struggle to survive?

I lean back, drumming my fingers on the table, trying to focus on strategy, on the threat the coven represents, but the pull toward her, the curiosity, the desire to understand her, gnaws at me, persistent and intense. Even here, in the command center of my pack, surrounded by order and discipline, she disrupts everything, and I'm powerless to stop it.

"Very well." I straighten in my seat, trying to regain an edge of control. "I understand your hesitancy. We'll just have to speak again when we know each other better." I rise from the table, and summon one of the guards outside the door. "Escort her back to her room," I say. "And keep post."

"Keep post?" Xamara's chair screeches across the floor as she stands. "You just apologized for kidnapping me, but you're still keeping me under lock and key?"

"I promise it's temporary." I take a step toward her, and she crosses to stand next to me, her arms folded beneath her chest. "I don't want you running off just yet. Not until I can ensure your safety." Her brow arches, but I don't flinch under her scrutiny; I can't. There's too much at stake. "You are being targeted," I continue, choosing my words carefully. "By the Nightborn. By the coven. Letting you roam free now would be dangerous for you and for all of us."

She scoffs and walks past me, ripping her eyes away from me. It stings more than a slash from the Nightborn.

As the guard escorts her toward the small room she was initially brought to, I curl my hands at my sides, a subtle manifestation of the pull to her that refuses to be ignored. It's irrational, even selfish, but I can't deny it. I long to see her again, to study the strength and fire in her, to hear her voice, to understand the way her mind works against the chaos of the world she's been dragged into.

I walk back into the war room to regain my composure, shutting the door behind me. Keeping her contained feels necessary–but wrong. I can't allow her to roam, not while the threat is real, yet every instinct I possess rebels at the notion of denying her freedom, even temporarily. It is a delicate balance of caution against desire, duty against longing. I sense, with a clarity that startles me, that the devastatingly beautiful woman who has so thoroughly captured my attention is more than a passing curiosity. She is a force, a presence that unsettles and fascinates me in equal measure.

I close my eyes briefly, letting the tension settle, knowing that for now, containment is the only prudent choice. The coven's shadow stretches wide, and Xamara of Moonfang must be protected.

I reach out to Lorna through the mind-link. *"Lorna, could you please meet with me in the war room?"*

Her response lands a heartbeat later. *"On my way, Alpha."*

I reclaim my seat and try to concentrate on the map on the table in front of me, but it's no use. I can't think of anything other than the girl.

A few moments later, the door swings open, and Lorna strides in. She shuts the door with her foot, her eyebrows already raised. "All right." She drops into the chair across from me. "What in the world is going on?"

I drag a hand across my jaw. "I need your advice."

"That much I gathered," she mutters. "What sort of mischief did you get yourself into this time?"

"I had the guard bring in a woman from the woods. Her name is Xamara, and she's... special."

She stares at me for a long moment and then bursts out laughing. "Oh, Moon Goddess, Alpha Julian. First rule: if you like a girl, don't abduct her."

I glare at her but feel the corner of my mouth twitch upward. "I didn't *mean to* abduct her. My men did not strictly follow my orders."

"Okay," she says dryly. "By *abducting her?*"

I pinch the bridge of my nose. "Lorna, what do I do? How can I get her to stay here willingly and not try to leave in the middle of the night without keeping her hostage?"

"Why must she stay? What exactly is the problem? Besides your terrible, terrible approach to courtship." She shakes her head and leans back in her chair.

Shaking my head, I insist, "I'm not courting her."

"Mm-hmm. And I'm not an alchemist." Lorna laughs under her breath. "So, what do you want?"

I hesitate at first but then say it plainly. "I want her to stay, but not because she's locked up, but because she chooses to."

"Well," Lorna says, "good news. You're not completely hopeless. Just mostly. Where is she right now?"

"She's in one of the small rooms where we keep political hostages...."

"Oh, Moon Goddess! Help me. All right, here's what you do." She straightens, her tone changing from teasing to practical. "If you want her to *want* to stay, start by treating her like a guest, not a prisoner. Prepare a bigger room, a nice room, Julian, not what's more or less a cell. Something warm, comfortable, and feminine. Give her something that feels safe, civilized, and peaceful. Make her feel valued. Let her take a warm bath and dress in a fine gown of her choosing."

I nod. This plan, at least, feels actionable.

"And then," she continues, "you sit down to have a meal with her. Not an interrogation. Not a strategy briefing. A *meal.* Talk to her like she's a person, not a problem to be solved."

"A meal?" I repeat. It makes sense, but the idea of sitting alone with her in such an intimate setting makes my breath catch in my throat.

"Yes, preferably one that doesn't seem like a negotiation between rival kingdoms. After that, you give her a choice: stay here as a guest… or you personally escort her wherever she wants to go."

Every muscle in my body tightens. I don't like the idea of letting her walk out of these doors, but Lorna's right.

"People don't choose cages," she says gently. "Even gilded ones."

I breathe out slowly. "Thank you, Lorna. I knew you'd know what to do."

"Of course I know what to do." She stands, still shaking her head. "You, however? You're a disaster."

I wouldn't let many other people talk to me this way, but we've known each other since we were pups, and besides Mason, Lorna is my best friend. "I'll manage."

She turns to walk toward the door. "Just try not to ruin it before sunset."

"I'll make sure everything's ready," I promise her.

Lorna turns to look at me, shaking her head, amusement dancing in her eyes. "Good luck, Alpha. You're going to need it." With that, she walks out, closing the door behind her.

"You're right about that," I murmur before opening the mind-link and sending orders to try to repair the damage I've already done.

11

POTENT, RARE, AND WILD

XAMARA

The door opens with a thud, far gentler than I expected, and I look up, surprised it's happening so soon. I've only been inside for a few minutes. A single guard stands in the doorway with a composed expression.

"Miss Xamara," he says, bowing his head. "Please come with me."

My pulse quickens, but I nod and follow. We walk through wide stone corridors that feel nothing like the woods or the rogue dens. These halls are warm, lit with golden sconces, the air fragrant with cedar and pine. Servants walk through the halls, their gazes moving over me, curiosity tempered by discipline.

I brace myself for judgment, suspicion, anything resembling the interrogation that usually follows being "escorted." Instead, the guard simply leads me deeper into the castle, and I wonder where we're going now.

We stop at a large set of wooden doors. He pushes one of them open, then steps aside. "Your new room, miss."

This isn't a cage—not even close.

Soft light from dozens of rose-scented candles pours across a chamber that looks like something out of a dream. Soft, blush-colored linens match the pink plush chairs. Deep rose-gold drapes shimmer when the breeze stirs them. I peek behind a door across the room and see a claw-foot bathtub sitting in the ensuite, steam curling lazily from its surface. The scent of lavender and eucalyptus hangs in the air.

Two maids bustle around, arranging and hanging gowns and towels, barely glancing at me except to offer gentle smiles.

"What is all this?" I manage.

"Your accommodations," the guard says simply. "By order of the Alpha."

I want to hold on to my irritation, to remind myself that I was just kidnapped and locked in a tiny room, but this suite makes it difficult. The warmth, the soft light, the quiet bustle of the maids, eases the tension I've been clinging to. It feels good to breathe without bracing for danger.

"Thank you." I turn and look directly at the guard. He nods once, then leaves.

The maids approach with the same polite respect. "We've prepared a bath for you, miss," one says. "And several gowns. You may choose whichever you like."

I shouldn't relax. I know better. Yet, when they guide me to the bath and help undo the ties of my borrowed tunic, I feel incredible relief–a reminder of what life is like when it isn't all claws, snow, cold, and running until my lungs nearly burst.

Warm water laps over my skin, and I sink beneath it with a sigh that escapes before I can hold it back. They wash my hair gently, as if I might break, and for a moment I forget the battle, the Nightborn, and the coven's shadow stretching toward me.

The maids introduce themselves as Cheryl, who is old enough to be my mother, and Renee, who is closer to my age. They are so kind, I suddenly feel at home here–not like someone who was captured and dragged here against her well.

After my bath, Cheryl brushes my hair while Renee laces the gown I've chosen, a simple green one with silk sleeves and a skirt that feels too soft to be real.

When the maids finish with the gown and step back, Cheryl opens the door with a polite nod.

"Alpha Julian said you may roam the castle freely, Miss Xamara–if and when you are ready."

My eyes widen in disbelief. What made him decide so suddenly to stop treating me like a prisoner? "Thank you both so much for your kindness," I say, looking from one maid to the other.

"It is our honor," Renee answers for both of them. Then, they bustle off, and I let out a deep breath, grateful to be alone.

I step out into the corridor, and I'm only a few steps from the doorway when voices drift from farther down the hall. It sounds like two staff members walking toward me, speaking freely.

"Of course, he still hasn't chosen a Luna. He's too busy saving the kingdom."

"Well, he'll have to eventually. Alphas can't stand alone forever."

"No one's caught his eye yet, I guess. And he long ago decided not to hold out for a fated mate. He's convinced he doesn't have one."

I pretend not to listen, but the words lodge in my mind. *An Alpha without a Luna.*

Two men round the corner. I step into an alcove, and they barely notice me as they walk by, though they do stop their conversation. Their clothing makes me think they are important–advisors to the Alpha, perhaps.

I wander down the hall, letting instinct guide me more than intention, until I come to a set of intricately carved double doors. Battle scenes are etched into the wood, along with wolves baring their teeth. The doors stand slightly ajar. Curiosity nudges me closer. I ease one open and find myself in a vast library. Rows of towering shelves stretch toward the ceiling, each packed with books. I can only imagine the tales of whimsy and history I can find here. The space is silent, not another soul here. Lantern light makes the polished tables glow.

I step inside, feeling at home here. I trail my fingertips lightly along spines until one catches my attention. It's a worn volume about territory histories. I take it to a corner table and lower myself into a chair. For a few minutes, I lose myself in the quiet, the book, and the strange feeling of being safe inside walls that don't belong to me.

I follow the lines of a river on the map, its dark ink twisting through forests and hills until it opens into a broad valley. The label reads Gleabhain River Valley. The label marking the territory there reads Blackwater Pack. Along the side of the page is a list of Alphas, all with the last name Abrenna. At the bottom, it says Julian Abrenna of Blackwater Pack.

I turn the page. Symbols, looping script, and warnings fill the margins, winding around maps of jagged mountains and deep forests. Notes mark certain peaks as forbidden, hinting of dangers that stretch back generations. Other passages speak of bloodlines and power, of forces hidden beneath the earth that are older than any pack or coven in Vaeloria, Hexeton, or the surrounding kingdoms. Each line pulses with a quiet authority, and the further I read, the deeper the intrigue burrows into me.

Maps of jagged mountains unfold across the next pages, etched in black and crimson, veins of arcane sigils running through the peaks. Curses or warnings, I can't tell, but each line sends a chill up my spine.

The final page makes me gasp: *Moonfang blood is potent, rare, and wild. It fuels hearts and stirs the spirit.*

Now, I understand why the Nightborn have hunted me so relentlessly. They seek my blood, and my white coat makes me a beacon.

Soft footsteps approach from behind me. I close the book and turn just as Julian steps into view.

"Miss Xamara," he says, his voice smooth. "I hoped I'd find you here."

I stand, smoothing the skirt of the emerald gown. "Your staff said I was free to wander the castle."

"You are." His gaze moves over my body, nothing improper, but enough to make my pulse quicken. "And I'm glad you chose the library."

"Oh? Is it one of your favorite rooms as well?"

"It is undoubtedly my favorite room in the castle. I've spent many hours here. I came to ask you, would you please join me for dinner?"

I take one last look around the library, letting my fingers hover over the spines of books I might never get the chance to open. I like this place, with its shelves packed with stories, maps, and secrets tucked into pages. It's a world of knowledge waiting to be discovered, but I *do* kind of like Julian as well, despite his faults. His deep brown eyes shine in a way that makes them almost impossible to look away from, and his upturned lips look so soft and warm. I wonder if they might be....

My stomach growls in hunger, but the pull to food is nothing compared to this other tug I'm feeling. A thrill at being near him ripples through me. I want to see what comes next.

"Of course, I'll join you for dinner." I keep my voice even but smile. "Thank you."

He nods and offers me his arm. We make small talk as Julian escorts me to the massive, elegant dining hall, where dozens of candles reflect light across polished silver. The long table could seat seventy, but only two places are set.

He pulls out my chair. "Here you are." His smile is warm and inviting.

I grin back at him and then settle into the chair. "Thank you, Alpha." My eyes meet his, and I allow just the faintest hint of amusement to show. "It seems the castle holds more wonders than I ever could have anticipated."

He lowers himself into the seat beside me, a small defiance of tradition that speaks of decency and thoughtfulness. I've seen many Alphas command a room, but never one willing to step back just to make someone else comfortable.

Servants glide in and out, setting plates before us. The food tastes incredible: roast, warm bread, soup, a potato dish I've never tried before, and vibrant vegetables.

As we are eating, Julian asks, "How do you like your new room?"

"It's beautiful and elegant. Thank you so much for your hospitality." I look into his eyes, and once again, my heart thumps erratically.

He meets my gaze. "I will not force you to stay here tonight." He takes a deep breath and continues. "If you wish, I will personally escort you wherever you need to go."

The offer is startling, but clearly genuine. He isn't trying to trap me. Nor is he asserting his power over me. He's giving me a choice. I find myself wanting to accept it for more than convenience.

"But it is late," he adds, his eyes moving toward the dim light outside the windows. "The sky has darkened, and the paths beyond these walls are not safe. I would appreciate you choosing to remain here tonight." His voice holds no demand, only a wish, a hope. "For your own safety."

I find myself nodding at him, despite how badly I want to get back to my friends. "Then I will accept."

He inclines his head, a faint but approving smile brushing his lips. "Wonderful." We finish eating our dessert, which consists of the most delicious apple pie I've ever had, and then he says, "I'll see you to your room."

We rise together, and I take his arm. The castle feels quieter now, the echoes of servants' footsteps much fainter with so many of them off-duty this time of evening.

Outside my door, Julian moves close enough that I can feel his breath on my cheek. His eyes linger on my lips. Butterflies flutter through me. I'm unsure and excited all at once. I wonder, for a split second, if he might kiss me, but he simply rests his hand on the door-knob. "Goodnight, Xamara." His voice is a whisper as he pushes the door open.

"Goodnight, Alpha." I try to keep the disappointment out of my voice when he nods and turns to walk away.

I step inside, letting the door close behind me. On the bed lies a nightgown, pale silver as moonlight, soft and inviting. I slide into it, the fine fabric brushing my skin.

Settling beneath the covers, I let the scent of lavender and fresh linens envelop me. My mind drifts, restless and alive. I wish I could reach my seven rogue friends through the mind-link. I want to hear their voices and let them know I'm safe and that I didn't just abandon them. I focus, doing my best to send a thought through the mind-link, but there's no answer.

But another current stirs within me. Thoughts of Julian swirl. I close my eyes and imagine his gorgeous eyes and the soft curve of his lips when he smiles. I wonder at the strength it must take to carry the mantle of Alpha King. How many battles has he already fought to protect his pack?

Night drapes over the castle, shadows dancing across the floor as the fire burns low, and I let sleep edge in. My last conscious thoughts jump wildly between Alpha Julian, the Nightborn, the looming threat of the coven, and the friends I can't reach.

1 2

READY FOR WAR

Julian

Xamara and I sit across from each other at the breakfast table, and I can't take my eyes off her. I'm mesmerized by the way her dark hair curls around her face, the radiance of her pale skin, the brilliant blue of her eyes, and the pout of her ruby red lips.

"This food is excellent," she says, her tone genuine. "And your home is magnificent. Thank you again for your hospitality." She sets her fork down, meeting my eyes. "I should tell you, though, I won't be staying here any longer. I need to find my friends so we can track the Nightborn, and eventually...." She hesitates for only a moment before finishing, "The coven itself."

I study her, thinking of how I've watched warriors fall, divisions scatter, armies crumble, but the determination in her voice is different. It isn't naïve; it isn't bravado. She knows what she's doing. She knows she has no protection beyond her own cunning, her own fangs and claws, and still, she vows to step into danger headfirst.

"I don't want you to face that alone," I insist. "I can provide warriors, resources, and strategists. You don't have to risk your life like this, not when my pack will stand with you. You will be stronger and safer with support."

Her expression softens into a polite, almost wistful smile. "I know you mean well," she says. "But we will manage on our own. I've only ever had bad experiences with armies."

I don't understand that, not entirely. She hasn't shared much of her past with me. But I do know she has survived more than most could bear, and her determination is formidable. But the thought of her moving through forests, valleys, and mountain passes, hunting creatures that feed on her blood, with nothing but her rogues beside her, is not something I can allow. Every instinct screams that she shouldn't be out there, that she shouldn't be risking herself without the advantage of preparation–and without the shield of my pack.

"I won't force you." The words taste bitter. I struggle to keep my tone even. "But you will need healers, information, and a firm plan. You can't do this blindly. If you'll let me–let us–help in any way, I will be there for you."

"I'm very grateful," she says. "And I appreciate your offer, Alpha, truly, but my path is my own."

She stands then, smooth, deliberate, composed. She thanks me again for the breakfast and the company. There's no anger, no defiance, only the careful politeness of a woman used to making her own way. I watch her move toward the door, and my heart clenches.

And then she's gone.

The click of the door seals the space she leaves behind. Silence stretches across the dining hall, unbroken except for the faint echo of her heels on stone. My stomach twists with frustration, helplessness, and longing.

I rise from my chair, devastation turning into something even fiercer: determination to keep Xamara safe. I can't let her walk into this danger unguarded. She can't face the Nightborn and the coven without a shield, without allies, and I can't stand idle while she risks her life.

I think of the bloodless sheep, of the Nightborn strikes, and of the power hiding in those mountains. Every calculation of risk, every thread of reason, points to one truth: she needs help, even if she refuses to admit it, and if she won't accept it willingly, I will find a way to ensure it–somehow.

She'll be out there, running toward enemies who will kill her without hesitation, and I won't let her go unprepared. Everything that hunts her has become my concern, and I will see her survive this as she runs through the rivers and forests that fall in or just outside of my pack lands. Her rogues are strong and fight well, but even they are not invincible.

I leave the dining room and take the main corridor, moving fast. The castle is quiet at this hour, so there's nothing to slow me as I cross the hall and step into the war room. Through the mind-link, I summon my Beta and most high-ranking warriors.

Moments later, the door opens and Mason steps in first, followed by Jax, Zara, Simeon, and Kai.

"The white she-wolf was here. We had a conversation about the Nightborn, and she left this morning." I manage to keep all emotion out of my voice. "Her name is Xamara of Moonfang. She's definitely the one the coven is after. She's moving alone now, searching for the seven rogue wolves."

Jax frowns, his jaw tight. "Alone? When the coven searches for her? That's... suicide."

"She's strong." I keep my tone firm. "But even the strongest fighter would be overwhelmed by the coven. That's why we are going to prepare. We control what we can–our pack, our warriors, and our readiness for war."

Kai crosses his arms, leaning back in his chair. "So what's the plan? Do we follow her? Try to intercept?"

I take a deep breath. "No direct interference. We prepare. We strengthen the pack. We send every warrior we can, so if she encounters danger, she has allies ready to strike, defend, and recover her. That will give us hundreds of warriors, all of them ready for anything."

Simeon rests his hands on the table. "Understood. When do we start?"

"Now," I command. She should be all right in the daylight, this early in the morning–I hope. We have time to prepare.

I send a message through the mind-link. *"Meet on the training field. Immediately."*

By the time we reach the designated location, wolves fan out in disciplined formations, their teeth bared. Jax and Simeon take opposite flanks, Mason and I anchor the center, Kai and Zara coordinate the younger wolves, ensuring that every movement is made with precision.

"We work on speed drills," I command through the mind-link. *"Get into pairs of four. Intercept hits, flank each other, attack, counter-attack, repeat. Anticipation without hesitation. Push past exhaustion. Every strike, every dodge, every movement must be instinctive and reflexive. There will be a time when you are too tired to think, and that's when adrenaline and muscle memory will save your life and your partners' lives."*

The pack erupts. Wolves twist, leap, collide, roll, and strike. Dust rises in clouds beneath claws. Growls and snapping teeth echo across the field. I weave among them, correcting movements, reassigning pairings, improvising obstacles, and forcing them to adapt mid-drill.

Even amidst the chaos, my mind maps patrol patterns, river routes, healing zones, and where to place recovery squads. Every calculation has her in mind–Xamara moving through forests and valleys, her soldiers at her side, and danger at every step.

Hours pass. When I finally stop and lift my head in a loud howl, hundreds answer in perfect unison. The pack is ready.

THE WOODEN DOOR CREAKS AS I STEP INTO LORNA'S CABIN, AND immediately the scent of dried herbs and hot wax fills the air. Torchlight streams over piles of books and glass vials that catch the light in rainbow sparks. Pots bubble quietly on the stove, the scent of juniper berries, patchouli, and vetiver mingling into a perfume of magic.

She stands near a table, her apron dusted with fine powders. Stray wisps of dark hair streaked with silver escape from the loose knot at the nape of her neck, framing a lovely face with bright eyes filled with mischievous intelligence. Her cheeks are slightly rouged from the heat of the stove and bubbling potions, and faint laugh lines crease the corners of her eyes. She tilts her head, one hand brushing back a stubborn strand of hair as she studies me with a mixture of curiosity and wry amusement. "Alpha Julian, how was your date?" she asks with a wink.

"It wasn't a date. Xamara left this morning, which is why I need your counsel." I fold my arms across my chest.

"Ah, yes. I thought she might have been more loyal to her friends than to us thus far... but, time will tell. Now, what can I do for you today, Alpha?"

"I need to know if it's even possible for you to conjure the sun to shine at night."

She raises an eyebrow, intrigued. "The sun at night?" She steps toward a wall lined with shelves, each crammed with bottles, jars, and scrolls tied with ribbons. "That is... *ambitious*, even for my taste."

"I know it is," I admit. "But I must know. Could you increase the reflection off the moon a fraction, enough to illuminate a battlefield or guide someone who's lost? I need to know if it's possible."

She traces her fingers over the spines of old leather-bound tomes until she pulls one from the shelf, the cover worn and etched with symbols that glow. She flips it open, muttering under her breath, scanning lines of runes and diagrams. "Hmm. I don't recall a spell quite like that. There are moonlight charms, fire orbs, lanterns that hold daylight   "

I step closer, letting my eyes sweep over the cabin: dried flowers hang from beams, tiny wind chimes tinkle above open windows, and shelves of bottles are filled with colored liquids. "Could one of those spells be adapted?"

Lorna hums thoughtfully, leafing through the pages meticulously. "I don't know. There are principles here that might apply, but the sun is not an energy that wants to be captured. Sunlight, sun heat, sun essence... to pull that into night, it could be dangerous. Or... unstable." She bites her lip, considering the consequences. "I'd need to do some *careful* experiments."

I nod. "Then try, but yes, be careful. I don't want you risking your life, Lorna."

She closes the book and places it on the table, gathering her vials and powders. "I'll see what I can do. I'll start with a small amount of light. If it holds, perhaps I can coax more." Her eyes gleam with the same playful curiosity I've seen in her all my life.

I take a step back, allowing her the space to work. "Very well. I'll leave you to it, then, and return once I've finished my other errands. I want to see the results."

My next stop is Helena, the healer. I slip into the *Apothecary Hollow*, a quiet section of the village where shifters come to heal and to be trained in the art of healing. The air is fragrant with the bittersweet tang of yarrow, the clean green aroma of plantain, and the gentle floral notes of calendula and chamomile.

Her home is much like Lorna's cabin. Glass vials collect dust on shelves, and bundles of dried comfrey, sage, and echinacea hang from the wooden rafters. A copper cauldron hisses in the corner, filled with a potion that's steam smells of mint. Open tomes lie on tables crowded with mortars and pestles, delicate brushes, and little bottles full of powdered root or flower petals that glint like crushed gems. Every corner of the home feels charged with care, study, and determination to heal.

Helena is crouched over a low table crowded with syringes and bandages. Her black, tightly coiled curls tumble around her face, framing pale skin and dark, attentive eyes that look up as I enter. "Alpha Julian," she says, setting down a jar. "I wasn't expecting you today."

"I should've announced that I was coming, but I need to ask you something important," I reply, moving closer. "How many healers do you have on your staff?"

"Twenty," she answers without hesitation. "All trained and very capable. Why?"

I take a deep breath, choosing my words carefully. "Helena, do you think you and your healers could learn the ways of battle? Could you train to fight?"

Helena looks at me like I've lost my mind, a furrow forming between her brows. "Learn to fight? Alpha Julian, why would we need to do that? We've always had plenty of warriors."

"I know it goes against a Blackwater healer's nature to do harm," I say, my tone low but firm. "However, there may come a time when I need my healers on the battlefield with the warriors. We would put you behind a safety line, but I want you there, Helena. On the back lines, ready to heal immediately. If a wolf falls, you patch them up, and they get right back into the fight. That keeps our numbers high, our strategy strong, and if the enemy comes for you, well, you'll need to be ready."

She tilts her head, processing the implications. Then, slowly, a small, approving smile spreads across her face. "That's a tremendous idea, Alpha. I hadn't thought of it that way. You're suggesting we not just heal after battle but maintain the pack's strength in real time, right?"

I nod. "Exactly. Speed, precision, and survival. The faster a warrior is back on their paws, the stronger the pack stays, and I trust you. I want you there, helping us win in ways only you can."

Her expression softens, but the spark of determination is unmistakable. "Then it will be done. We'll start learning. The next time you call the training session, my staff and I will come to the field."

I allow myself a brief smile. "Good. I'll see you there, then. And Helena, thank you. Your work is more important than you realize."

She nods. "We'll be ready. Don't worry, Alpha Julian. My staff and I adapt quickly under pressure."

I leave the hollow with a renewed sense of purpose. The pack is ready; the warriors are ready, but now, the healers will be, too. When the next battle comes, we'll move as one: warriors, healers, and strategy intertwined, all working to keep Xamara and the pack alive.

13

NO TIME FOR JOKES

I shift at the edge of the Blackwater Pack castle's tree line, snow white fur springing from skin, muscles rippling beneath, my paws sliding into the earth with a perfect grip. The wind cuts across my muzzle, carrying the scent of winter-pine, river water, and decaying leaves. My ears twitch when I lift my head and break into a sprint. Sunlight blazes all around me, and my heart is pounding against my ribcage.

The map inside the book in Julian's library is sealed in my memory, with its rough markings giving me a vague sense of where my friends live.

I try again through the mind-link, nudging into the invisible threads of their thoughts, straining my mind across mountains and forests. *"Havelock? Seamus? Ian? Mac? Willow? Lark? Ivy?"*

No one answers. The forest buzzes and chirps around me. The distant call of birds and the rustle of leaves are clear, but there's still nothing through the mind-link. For hours and hours, I run through the woods, searching for my friends.

When the woods start to look more familiar, I push harder,

reaching as far as I can with my mind as I weave through the trees. *"Havelock!"* I shout.

I still don't hear anything, but the sense that I've been heard settles over me. It has to be Havelock in the distance. Relief floods through me. Then I hear a familiar voice, almost a growl.

"Finally."

Exhilaration sparks within me. They can hear me! I race, calling through the mind-link, urgency in every pulse. *"Havelock! Seamus! Ian! Mac! Willow! Lark! Ivy! I'm here! Guide me to you!"*

Ian's voice fills my mind, his tone playful. *"It's about time, Xamara. We thought we lost you."*

I let out a sigh. *"You almost did."*

A calm presence, Lark's voice, comes through the mind-link, *"I smell you, Xamara. You're just east of us. Keep moving this way. Don't stray, and we'll meet you at the ridge. We're almost there."*

I race ahead, and when the trees finally thin, I see my friends ahead. My muscles relax in a way they haven't since I was taken. I'm so grateful to be reunited with them.

"There you are!" Havelock's deep voice says in my thoughts. *"Where have you been?"*

"I was taken," I send sharply, letting the words cut through the mind-link. *"Alpha Julian of Blackwater Pack had me taken, and I stayed overnight in his castle."*

Ian's tone is filled with outrage. *"That bastard! He's lucky his men didn't run into us."*

Willow speaks softly, concern threading through her tone. *"Are you hurt? Did he do anything to you?"*

"No," I reply. *"He was actually very considerate and quite good company."*

Ivy weaves playfully around me. If a wolf's face could look skeptical, that would be the expression she's giving me now. Still, she does not comment on my last remark. *"You gave us a scare. Don't disappear on us again!"*

Mac trots up close, his chestnut fur brushing my side. *"I'm glad you're back, but it's almost sunset. We need to make a plan. Do we go home or seek out the coven tonight?"*

Havelock's deep voice cuts through the mind-link. *"I say we move tonight. The coven is closer than home. We should at least get a clear idea of what we're up against."*

Willow speaks next. *"I second that. The Nightborn are thicker near the river. We can avoid them if we circle east first."*

Ian chimes in. *"Keep our formation tight, and watch for traps."*

One by one, the rogues voice their agreement through the mind-link. We hunt the coven tonight. The plan is set.

All of us sprint through twisted ridges, dense trees, and rocky slopes. The river churns ahead, the last rays of sun glinting off its surface. With synchronized leaps, we cross, water lapping against our fur. On the far bank, the mountain range rises.

"We're almost there," Lark says through the mind-link. *"The mountains are just beyond the next rise."*

The forest thins, and stony cliffs rise like guardians. We press forward. The wind carries a faint scent of smoke and iron, a warning of what waits ahead.

Finally, the cavern mouth yawns before us, its jagged opening swallowing the last streaks of sunlight. We slip inside, moving silently over the stone. The air is thick, heavy with magic, tingling against our fur. Shadows dance along the walls, moving with the glow of torches.

And there they are. Cloaked figures circle a dark, writhing source at the center, chanting low, power radiating outward. My nose twitches and my ears raise as I pause to observe. The rogues fan out, flanking me instinctively in silent acknowledgment. They reassure me that we have strength in numbers, and all of us are skilled fighters.

"So this is the coven?" Mac asks. *"There are so many of them. No wonder the darkness has spread so far."*

Havelock replies, *"We need to rethink attacking. We are not prepared for so many. Watch and learn, and then we will retreat and make a plan."*

Everyone agrees with his assessment. Attacking so many witches seems like an awful idea, given how many of them there are and how few of us.

I fix my eyes on the inner circle. Cloaked heads dip in synchronized rhythm, chanting in a language as old as the mountains. Power hums in the stone beneath my paws, curling into my senses, dark and alluring. One figure, tall, pale, unmistakably familiar, stands at the center. I gasp. Step by step, the truth settles in: My stepmother, Luna Selvara, is leading them, weaving her black power into the ritual.

The ritual itself is mesmerizing but vile. Candles burn in unnatural colors–deep violet that seems to swallow light, black that absorbs everything, red that slithers in slow motion like blood. The smoke from them curls and stretches unnaturally, crawling toward the outer edges, licking the cave floor with spectral fingers.

My stepmother's hands move over a cauldron of black water, swirling it so that the reflection ripples into visions of pain, loss, and creatures half-formed, red eyes glinting from voids of shadow. Her lips move in a soft, melodic chant, sending waves of power through the cave, feeding the energy spiraling around the inner circle.

With a shudder, I signal the rogues subtly, and they tighten around me. Our tails are low, and every muscle is tense, our ears flicking. Each of them feels the weight of the magic, the pull of danger, and yet their presence steadies me. I am furious, trembling with betrayal, but the rogues' vigilance allows me to witness it fully, to mark every movement of the coven without alerting them.

Every gesture, every word, every pulse of magic is a dark, evil hypnosis so malevolent I can taste it on my tongue and feel it in the fur along my spine.

I reach out through the mind-link. *"Let's get out of here before they see us."*

Without a word, the eight of us slowly slink out of the cave, keeping our paws light until we're at a safe distance. And then we run.

Once we're a safe distance away, I say, *"It's her. Luna Selvara, my stepmother. The one who cast you out."*

Every eye widens in shock and surprise. They look at one another and then return their attention to me. Havelock speaks first, steel and anger in every word. *"I thought I recognized her, the witch at the top of the coven. The bitch kicked us out, and now she's using her powers for evil."*

Seamus's tone holds a tight edge to his usual mischief. *"The evil has been hiding in plain sight this whole time."*

"Yes," I reply, grinding my teeth in frustration. *"She lied to my father. She told him she was just a shifter. The Moonfang Pack trusted her, but she was a witch all along. All of it was a lie. Now, my father is dead, and she's the leader of the pack and the coven, commanding the Nightborn and weaving black magic. I never imagined...."*

Willow chimes in. *"I recognized her energy before we even saw her. She cast us out because we called her on her mistreatment of others as Luna. She's been manipulating every one of us."*

"She exiled us when we started to notice discrepancies in her story and the mistreatment of her pack members," Ivy says. *"There's betrayal woven into every step of her life."*

"Agreed," I add. *"She's been a liar, a manipulator, and she's been shaping events from the shadows, but now we know. And that knowledge is power."*

Ian flicks his tail, his tone sardonic despite the tension. *"Family drama just hit maximum levels. Stepmother, caster of spells, liar extraordinaire."*

I shake my head, finding humor in his conclusion, despite the situation.

"We need to move carefully." Willow's tone is full of concern. *"We must protect each other at all costs. Let's go home and prepare. She may be powerful, but she isn't invincible, not with us linked and aware."*

Agreement threads through the mind-link, every rogue's resolve a tether of shared anger and purpose. The betrayal cuts deep, but the unity of my friends steadies me. We are wolves in shadows, bound by blood, fury, and a common goal. Together, we will find a way to defeat her.

We move as one, melting through the shadowed trees, our hearts pounding in sync. The revelation of Luna Selvara's true nature hangs between us. Every rogue beside me is tense, their ears twitching, bodies low to the ground, scanning the area for any sign of danger.

We are nearly home when a shriek slices through the trees–high, piercing, inhuman–and the forest erupts around us. Bodies hurl themselves out of the shadowed treetops, red eyes blazing, the sound of their claws ripping through brush echoing like tearing fabric. The air vibrates with their screeches as they flood the clearing from every direction at once, too many shapes, too many teeth, closing too fast. The ground quakes beneath the force of their charge, and before any of us can brace, one slams into my side, turning the world into snarls, snapping jaws, and chaos.

"Attack!" Ian shouts through the mind-link.

I launch forward before the next one fully lands, slamming into the Nightborn hard enough to crack bone, my jaws locking around its throat as its scream gurgles out. Blood spatters the rocks beneath us. Around me, the rogues form a ring. Havelock plows through the front line like a living battering ram. Seamus darts in quick flashes of blond fur to slash anything that gets close. Willow tears into one that lunges for my flank, but I am already breaking free, already attacking again, ripping another Nightborn off Ian's back before it can sink its teeth into his flesh. The world narrows to claws, fangs, and instincts, and I refuse to fall.

Ivy and Lark flank me, weaving agile strikes, their fur shimmering faintly in the low light. Mac dances between the Nightborn, his chestnut coat flashing as he drives them back with cunning feints. I hurl myself into the opening they create, slamming my weight into a Nightborn that slips through their guard, my fangs tearing into its shoulder. It shrieks, buckling under me as I drag it down. My claws rake through it until it stops thrashing and turns to ash. Another lunges from the side, but I spin, my paws blood-slick, brace, and rip its wing in half before its claws even touch my fur.

Yet, they continue to come in waves, and they're so fast. They're too hungry for my blood. Fangs tear at my flank; claws rake my shoulders. Pain blooms in flashes, and the taste of iron fills my mouth. Blood seeps freely from shallow cuts and deep gashes. My strength falters, and my pulse slows.

"Xamara!" Havelock yells, but I can't respond. My legs tremble, my muscles failing. The mind-link strains as the rogues continue to fight, but my vision narrows, darkness pooling at the edges.

"Hold on," Willow says, but I can't hold on. My consciousness

wavers as the Nightborn press in, relentless and cruel. The smell of blood mixes with their acrid stench. I feel fangs tear at my neck, claws scrape my sides, and then... darkness.

Even in the blackness, I feel them around me. The rogues are still fighting, still defending, still tethering me to life through their determination, but my body has failed me. The world goes quiet, and I slip away completely.

14

EMBRACE THE NIGHT

Julian

I sit at the edge of the training yard, watching Helena move among the healers as they run through drills in wolf form. They are learning to defend themselves, practicing blocks, strikes, and stances while keeping their focus on protecting the wounded. Helena mirrors Mason's movements. She's hesitant at first, testing her own ability to fight, but she improves with each repetition under my Beta's instructions.

The ground beneath my feet rattles, smoke curling the air. Everyone freezes and looks up. I hold up a hand to reassure everyone, seeing a puff of black trailing from the tower of the castle where the alchemists are hard at work. "Lorna," I mutter, shaking my head.

Helena lets out a deep breath and nods. The drills continue with the occasional magical mishap nearby.

Movement at the edge of the training yard catches my eye. I turn to see my patrols returning, escorting a group of unfamiliar wolves. My breath catches in my throat as I scan the strangers. Is Xamara with them? I believe these are the rogues she's been living with. I don't see her.

The leader of the group, an older warrior named Nash, speaks through the mind-link. *"Alpha, I recognized these wolves. They seem to mean us no harm. I'm bringing them to you so they can explain themselves."*

I study the approaching figures, noting their posture, and the alertness in their eyes. Something has happened. Perhaps Xamara didn't get back to them. I sent a patrol to trail her, but she's fast. Is it possible she slipped away from them?

Keeping my composure, I reply, *"Understood,"* and wait for them to reach me.

The seven rogues draw closer, cautious but unafraid, and I prepare myself to hear what they have to say.

As they near the edge of the training yard, I raise a hand. "One of you," I say, "go to the barracks, shift, dress, and return. The rest of you will remain here in your wolf."

The largest, a black wolf, follows one of my guards into the barracks. The six remaining wolves sit in the yard, showing their submission.

A large man with hair the same color as his dark fur emerges from the tent. He approaches me with narrowed eyes, his eyebrows knit together. It's clear he's wary of me, and I suppose I can't blame him. Their trust has clearly been broken by royalty before.

I incline my head. "What is it? Where's Xamara?" I command.

"We were attacked by the Nightborn," he begins, his gruff voice a low growl. "She was their target."

Taking a deep breath, I still myself for news I'm not sure I can bear to hear. "Go on."

"They drained her blood until she lost consciousness. We did our best to wake her, but then… witches appeared out of the woods. They used their magic to disable us. While she was out, the witches lifted her into the air, shifted her to human form, wrapped her in an ivory gown, and took her with magic we couldn't break. We couldn't reach her, and we can't fight them alone."

Taking a deep breath, I go over everything he's told me. At least she's alive–for now. "The witches have Xamara?"

"Yes. They took her to a cavern. They're using her blood to fuel their dark power." He folds his massive arms across his chest.

"Did the Nightborn let you follow them?"

"They left us alone once she was theirs. We tried to intervene, but the coven's power was too great." The defeat in his voice is evident. I feel it in my chest.

Still, I have to focus. All is not lost yet. "You followed them? You know their location?"

"We tracked her to the caves. We saw enough to know the ritual they're performing. Xamara's stepmother is among the witches. She is Luna Selvara of Moonfang. We watched her lead the group. She's a liar and a vampiric witch. We realize we need an army and hoped you'd help. We'll guide you to her." He raises his chin and awaits my decision.

Without hesitation, I issue the commands, my voice carrying over the training field. "Mason, split the warriors into two squads. One holds the perimeter here, ready to engage any Nightborn that may attack our packmates. The other follows the rogues to the caves."

The warriors obey immediately, shifting into motion without hesitation. I move to the edge of the field and shift. A howl tears from my throat, sharp, commanding, a signal that echoes across the territory. My pack answers immediately, a chorus of fury and loyalty as hundreds of black wolves nearly identical to mine move out.

The rogues take off on the path to the cavern, and my pack surges forward, following behind them.

We crash through the forest in a wave of fur and paws, the ground trembling beneath us. Branches whip past, snapping and tearing, but no one slows. The air is thick with the coppery tang of blood and the acrid smoke of dark magic, every sense on edge. We run for hours into the darkness until the cavern mouth appears ahead, jagged stone framed by shadow, a white glow seeping from within.

The rogues fan out around me as we approach, ears alert, noses twitching, our bodies low to the ground. The black wolf who led the way pauses at the threshold. The others press close behind, silent but ready.

The Nightborn cling to the cave ceiling like a swarm of bats.

Hundreds of them, their eyes glowing red in the torchlight, watch with a predatory precision, their fangs bared, all focused on Xamara.

Suspended mid-air in a shimmer of pale light, she hangs in human form, wearing a flowing white dress, her black curls floating around her like a dark halo. She's unconscious yet unmistakably alive. Her chest rises and falls, her forehead creased in discomfort. She's still beautiful even in slumber, even with dark tendrils of magic spiraling from the witches toward her.

I lock my eyes on her. My heart pounds, fury flowing through my veins. The witches' power radiates through the cavern, crackling and twisting, but it is her life, the woman I can't lose, that consumes my every thought.

Their chant cuts through the winter night. It rises from the circle of cloaked figures at the center, their hands raised and bodies swaying in a dark rhythm that drips with malice. Evil power rolls off the witches in waves, making the fur on my neck stand on end.

They command the Nightborn above, every movement bending the creatures to their will. The coven's magic is tangible and cruel. The wrath inside me coalesces with every beat as they chant:

Blood of Moonfang, blood of night,
Bind the shadows, burn out the light.
Vampiric kin, we serve your quest
Moonfang blood shed on moonlit crest
Crimson power, bloodlust bold,
Drink, obey, do as foretold.
Fangs, claws, Moonfang name,
Carry forth black spirit's claim.
Power of blood and loyal bite,
Awake, arise, embrace the night.

The Nightborn drop from the cavern ceiling one after another. Each descends toward Xamara with predatory precision, fangs glinting in the torchlight. I grit my teeth, watching in fury as the first sinks its fangs into her neck, the shimmer of enchanted light dimming as her blood is siphoned away. Another follows, then another, the line of pale, red-eyed creatures methodical in their feeding, taking her blood in turns.

I can't watch her suffer another second. Rage rips through me, scorching every nerve. I lunge forward, my claws flashing and my teeth bared. I let a howl tear from my throat; it's not a warning, but a call to battle.

Through the mind-link, I reach every warrior: *"Strike now with no hesitation. Protect her!"*

The air explodes around us as my pack surges and the rogues cut toward the witches' circle. The cavern trembles with the clash of magic and claw when my warriors meet the coven head-on. The rogues fan out, striking with lethal precision, weaving between enemies, teeth and claws tearing, bodies flashing under torchlight. The witches scream, their chants breaking into frantic shouts as our fury crashes into them, unstoppable and relentless. I carve a path through the dark power, every heartbeat driven by my need to reach Xamara, every movement a promise: She will survive, and every witch who dared touch her blood will pay with their lives.

The Nightborn swoop from above us in a shrieking, tearing rain of claws and wings. They crash into us like a storm of bone and shadow, their screams slicing through the cavern as they swarm my warriors and the rogues. I snarl and tear one from the air, ripping it apart, but three more slam into Mason, dragging him back. Above us, the witches rise, lifted by their own magic, floating higher and higher until they're out of our reach. Their robes whip in the unnatural wind as they continue the ritual. Their voices spiral in the fevered chant. Power crackles across the ceiling like lightning. The Nightborn fight with a frenzy I've never seen, driven by the coven's command, and we are forced back into a brutal, suffocating melee beneath the hovering witches. Their cold, triumphant laughter bounces against the stones as the battle blazes around me.

One by one, the witches descend from their hovering heights, gliding toward Xamara with a predatory grace. Each sinks their teeth into her, drinking, and instantly the wounds they carried from my warriors' strikes vanish as her blood courses through them. Cuts seal, bruises fade, muscles tighten; her power heals them, fuels them, and something darker than magic blooms in their eyes.

They truly aren't just witches; they are vampires, bound to her blood, feeding not only on her life but on the extraordinary power it contains. The shimmer of Xamara's vitality flickers, tethered to their predation, and I feel my anger spike, burning hot in my chest. I have to stop them before they drain her completely.

The Nightborn continue their assault, ripping through the cavern and lunging for any wolf in range, but my gaze is fixed on her, on the cruel elegance of the vampire-witches drawing from her, feeding, thriving. Every second they drink, they grow stronger, younger, more untouchable, and I know this is why they want her. Their immortality, their power, is bound to her blood. She is the center of it all, and I refuse to let them have her.

That's when I see the purple wolf jump up on a cliff inside the cave. Violet fog coils around her as she growls, using her magic to try to take down the witches, but they're too strong. Still, it's enough to scare them, and one by one they retreat higher into the cave.

The last witch shrieks, her fangs bared, and in an instant, the coven twists, turning into black bats. They rise, flitting like shadows against the torchlight, leaving the cavern in a swirl of bat wings and cruel magic.

Xamara drops.

I lunge instinctively, diving beneath her. She lands on me softly, impossibly light. Her dress fans around us, a white flower in the darkness, her black hair brushing against my muzzle.

I howl at the unfairness, at the betrayal, at the thought that this might be the last time I ever touch her.

If she dies, I will never get the chance, never even once, to kiss her, to taste what I might have begged the Moon Goddess to allow.

Her body is limp as I slide from beneath her. She's trapped under the dark spell that still curls like smoke around her. I circle protectively, growling to warn the Nightborn lurking above. I beg the Moon Goddess for mercy, but Xamara doesn't wake. Did the witches abandon her because she's drained completely and is about to breathe her last, or can my healers save her?

The battle rages around me, warriors and rogues locked in a deadly war with the Nightborn, but I can't tear my focus from her. I shift into human form, quickly pulling pants from the pack I always wear. Every instinct screams at me to be careful, that I'm more vulnerable in my human form, but Xamara is all that matters. I'm so drawn to her that I *need* to feel her lips on mine–before she slips away forever, and nothing, not even the madness of this fight, will stop me.

I lower my head, pressing my lips to hers. The chaos of the cavern fades, the Nightborn screams and the clash of fur and teeth are reduced to nothing. The fleeting warmth of her in my arms is all that exists. One kiss, one stolen, desperate moment, and I hold on to it as if it could last forever, even knowing she may never wake, and my heart is broken.

15

DIAMONDS, BLOOD, AND ASH

I stand inside a warm room, my eyes fixed on a woman holding a baby in her arms. Through the window, snow drifts silently against the glass, glinting in the sunlight.

The woman's black hair falls in soft waves around her face. Her pale skin is luminous, and her bright sapphire blue eyes catch mine. She's impossible to look away from. Her deep blue gown matches the color of her eyes, and that's when I realize the woman is my mother, and the baby cradled in her arms is me.

My mother looks down at me as a baby and says, "The snow outside sparkles like diamonds. Xamara—that shall be your name. It means 'diamond,' and you, my little one, will sparkle all your life."

I watch my mother's face, memorizing it, aching at the warmth in it.

The moment holds until a sharp crack slices through the air.

The dream tears apart, and Julian's lips are on mine.

I taste the desperation in his kiss as if he thinks he's lost me. I blink a few times, looking up at him, trying to remember what is happening.

The cave shakes with the violence around us, wolves and Night-

99

born bodies slamming into stone, but for one second all I feel is Julian. For one second, I'm safe.

He lifts his head and breathes hard, his eyes burning. His forehead crinkles when he realizes my eyes are open. "Xamara," he whispers, relief cutting through the noise. Then, sharper, he adds, "You're awake. Thank the Goddess. Can you shift?"

There's no time to reply, no time to think. I shift in a single breath. Bones crack and reshape. Fur plumes across my skin. Julian shifts beside me just as fast, his black wolf towering over mine in the dim cave light.

He nods toward the exit, and I take off running. He follows.

The cave is sheer chaos as black wolves crash into the Nightborn, rogues scrambling through the mess, bodies slamming into the enemy. The space is tight and the air is acidic with the scent of blood.

A Nightborn swoops down, its wings cutting through the air. Claws reach for me, but Julian lunges with his teeth snapping through its dark flesh, and drives it away. I don't stop to look. He pushes me forward, forcing a path toward the far tunnel.

"This way," he says in my mind. Why I can hear him when he's from another pack, I don't know, but again, I cannot stop to question it now.

I follow him, my paws slipping on stone slick with mud and blood. The cave quakes from bodies colliding and Nightborn crashing through the space above us. One of them slams into the wall inches from my head, sending chunks of rock flying.

Even though my head is swimming, and I feel a bit dizzy, we don't slow.

Julian darts left to block a Nightborn that is lunging for me, taking the hit across his chest but driving his shoulder into it hard enough to send it crashing into a boulder. He won't let anything touch me.

"We're almost there," he tells me, leading me toward the narrow passage where there's an exit. *"Keep going."*

We burst through the last stretch of tunnel and into the cold night air. Beyond the cave mouth, the forest is blurry. The instant we clear the stone threshold, Julian's voice threads through my mind again. *"Stay right beside me."*

"I'm here," I assure him, keeping pace, and the further we get from the cave, the more my thoughts finally catch up. *"Julian... what is happening? How can we hear each other in the mind-link? How did we get to that cave? Am I still dreaming?"*

His answer is immediate, clipped but controlled. *"The witches put you to sleep. They need your blood. It fuels their magic. It amplifies it. Without it, they're much weaker. With it, they're deadly."*

We break through a line of underbrush into a hollow shielded by fallen trees and jagged rocks. The forest around us is quiet here, the snow muffling every sound, giving us a moment to breathe.

My side brushes against his. The cave is far behind, but my heart still races. He didn't answer all of my questions. I look at him with wide eyes, waiting.

"My kiss woke you. It pulled you out of the spell," he whispers through the mind-link.

"I felt you," I answer. *"Our bond is what brought me back."*

"We are fated mates, Xamara. That's why we can speak like this. That's why I could reach you when nothing else could."

Distant echoes of the battle pulse through the trees, muted but unmistakable. Snow drifts onto Julian's dark fur as he turns his head toward the sound, every line of his body sharpening with tension. I feel it through the bond, too, his fear for our people, the pull to return, the instinct to fight.

"They need us," I say.

Julian's amber eyes meet mine. *"I wanted to get you to safety, but they can't finish this without us."*

"We're not running away," I tell him. *"I know you want to protect me, but we can help."*

"We'll go back, but stay close to me."

I take a deep breath and nod, and then, we launch back toward the battle.

The cave is alive with mayhem, but the Nightborn are faltering.

Warriors and rogues slam into the last of them, fangs tearing, claws slicing.

I run beside Julian, our movements synced, our bond threading every motion. A Nightborn swoops down, and Julian lunges. His teeth snap through its flesh, sending it crashing into a wall. I pivot as the next one charges Havelock, who swipes it aside with a growl of pure strength. I claw at it, knocking it into the wall.

"Xamara!" Havelock's voice hits my mind, firm but relieved. *"You didn't need to risk your life by coming back. We've almost finished them."*

"I'm here," I send back, my fangs revealed, my fur tufted. *"I will fight beside you. We will finish this together."*

Seamus darts past. *"Seriously, Xamara, you scared us half to death! But thank the Moon Goddess you're awake and alive."*

A monstrous Nightborn claws toward Ivy, and I intercept it mid-leap. My teeth sink into its side. Julian shakes the next one in his jaws. Every movement is instinct, every turn and pounce choreographed through the bond that ties us.

Lark circles an injured Nightborn, her lavender fur blending with shadows. Before the creature can strike, she and Willow pounce on it together, turning it to ash.

Mac throws his body against a Nightborn that tries to pin Ian. Ian turns his head and snaps its neck with precision. One by one, the remaining Nightborn crumble, reduced to ash that drifts like black snow onto the cavern floor.

The last Nightborn screams, flinging itself at Julian and me simultaneously. We collide with it as one. Teeth and claws shred its body, turning it into dust. Silence falls. The cave is still, except for ragged breathing and the remaining dust particles trickling from above.

"Xamara, why did you come back?" Ivy whispers through the mind-link, trembling slightly with relief. *"We had this under control."*

"And we finish it together," I answer, my fur brushing against Julian's as we move through the settling ash.

He presses his shoulder to mine. *"They're gone,"* he murmurs. *"We protected each other."*

"I won't ever be worried about my safety again as long as we can fight every battle like this," I tell him. *"Side by side?"*

Amber eyes meet mine, trust and loyalty reflected in the bond. *"I promise I'll never leave you again,"* he replies.

Warriors, rogues, Julian, and I stand together in the dark cave flowing with blood and ash, victorious and alive.

But the witches are still out there.

16

I'M YOURS

XAMARA

The castle is alive with laughter, overflowing glasses, and buzzing conversation, the warmth of the fires chasing away the chill from the snow outside. I move through the great hall, taking in the Blackwater Pack banners and glowing candlelight, the scent of roasted deer and sweet berry pies drifting from the kitchens. Everywhere I look, warriors and rogues mingle. The Nightborn are defeated, their shadows vanquished, yet the witches' escape leaves a gnawing unease at the edge of my mind.

Julian stands near the center of the room, talking quietly with two of his packmates. The familiar pull of the bond draws me closer. I weave between rogues and warriors alike to reach him.

I glance over and catch Seamus and Willow, their hands brushing as they move together. She leans in just enough to make him smile, and he doesn't step back. The way they interact is playful and unmistakably flirtatious.

Havelock and Ian laugh loudly at something Mac has said, and Ivy talks with one of Julian's warriors, flashing him her prettiest smile. Lark stands near the drinks table with an older woman from Blackwater Pack, deep in what appears to be a serious conversation.

I wait at the edge of the small circle, letting Julian finish speaking with his warriors. When he turns toward me, his expression softens, a small smile tugging at the corners of his mouth. "Xamara," he says, "are you hungry? The chefs have prepared a huge feast to celebrate our victory." I take a step closer, relieved at the normalcy in his tone, and fall into step beside him as we move toward the table ladened with food.

I look up at him. "All of this smells amazing."

Julian lifts his hand, and the hall falls silent. "Tonight, we celebrate more than the defeat of the Nightborn," he begins, his voice strong. "We celebrate courage, unity, and the bonds that have carried us through impossible odds. Each of you, warrior and rogue alike, has shown what it means to fight not just for yourselves, but for each other. Let this night be a reminder that together, we are unstoppable. Feast, laugh, and honor those who fought beside you. The victory we share tonight belongs to all of us, and the strength we share will carry us through until we find the coven and destroy the witches once and for all."

Everyone cheers, and then we all fill our plates and dig in. Julian's pack and the rogues share food, stories, and relieved smiles, the tension from the battle slowly fading. I watch the crowd, fascinated, noticing how easily the rogues blend in with the warriors and pack members of Blackwater.

Once most have finished eating, the music swells, drawing attention to the open floor. Willow moves with Seamus, their steps light and effortless, her laughter ringing out as he spins her around the floor. There's something tender in the way he watches her, a careful attentiveness that makes the small spark between them impossible to ignore. I can't help but smile at the moment, which is a stark contrast to the violence and fear that had dominated our lives only hours before.

Ivy finds a partner from Blackwater and moves with assured grace, while Ian dances with a female warrior.

Lark is still sitting with the striking older woman near the edge of the hall, her expression animated as they converse. Curious, I glance at Julian. "Who's that woman over there with my friend Lark?" I ask.

He nods toward the pair, his voice calm but warm. "That's Lorna, my alchemist. She brews potions that can conjure weather, mend wounds, strengthen our spirits, and even shift the tide of a fight."

"Ah, no wonder she and Lark are fast friends."

Julian smiles at me, then extends his hand. "She was in the thick of things during the battle, the healers helping the wounded so they could get right back into the fight. That's why we didn't lose anyone."

My eyes widen. I've never heard of such a thing. "That's remarkable."

A new song begins. "May I have this dance?" Julian asks with a grin pulling up one corner of his mouth.

Laughing, I slip my hand into his, and he leads me onto the floor. We move together easily. The new song is softer and slower. Julian pulls me closer, and I feel a flutter of happiness and safety in his arms.

When the song ends, he looks at me with a devilishly handsome smile. "Please, come with me," he murmurs, and I follow as he makes his way to the center of the hall. He asks me to call the rogues forward, and one by one, they step up, their expressions a mix of curiosity and anticipation.

Julian's voice is loud and clear. "Each of you fought bravely and deserves a place here. You'll each have rooms of your own in Abrenna Castle. You are welcome to make our pack your new home."

They exchange glances of gratitude. "Thank you so much, Alpha," Havelock says on behalf of all of my friends.

Julian nods to each of them before turning his attention back to me. "Xamara," he whispers. "I'd like you to join me on the balcony above the castle grounds. There's a view you shouldn't miss."

I nod, my pulse quickening as he takes my hand again, leading me up the spiral staircase, away from the celebration below, toward the promise of something more private.

On the balcony, the sounds of the party drift up from the hall, but we are finally alone together. Snowflakes flutter past us, catching the light from the torches below. Julian's eyes meet mine, intimate, intense, and for a moment everything else fades. He leans closer, and I feel the magnetic pull between us.

Our lips meet tentatively at first, a brush of curiosity and longing, then more urgently and consuming. I rest my hands lightly on his shoulders and lose myself in the warmth of his body against mine.

When we finally part, I rest my forehead against his chest, laughing softly. "I can't believe I missed our first kiss because I was asleep," I murmur.

He looks at me with a teasing smile. "That's okay. We have plenty of time to make up for it."

I realize Julian shifted mid-battle just to kiss me. Awe and gratitude fill me as I take in the magnitude of that sacrifice, changing into human form just to share that one kiss with me.

A wave of emotion crashes over me, and I lift up on my toes to press my lips to his again. This time, there's no hesitation, no shyness, just the raw connection between us, the realization of everything he's done for me and everything we've been through already. It's just the two of us and the snowflakes falling from the night sky.

When we finally part, Julian keeps his hand on me. "Would you like to continue this somewhere even more private?" he asks, his voice low.

I nod, my heart pounding. "Yes, I would."

He takes my hand, and we descend the stairs and make our way through the castle corridors until we reach his quarters. He closes the door behind us, and our lips meet again. The kiss deepens, and I press my body closer to his, exploring the contours of his broad shoulders and muscular chest.

My fingers trail along the hem of his tunic, the warmth of his skin beneath calming me. I undo his buttons, slowly revealing the planes of his chest. Each motion is an exchange of trust, desire, and anticipation building between us.

I slide my hands over his biceps, feeling the taut muscle beneath my fingers. A rush of desire sparks between us. He finds the front laces of my gown, loosening them slowly until the fabric slips from my shoulders, revealing my breasts. He buries his mouth in my neck, trailing kisses down to my collarbone, his fingers brushing over my nipples, teasing me until I gasp.

My hands wander lower, and I feel his hard cock through the fabric of his trousers. A shiver runs through me at the realization of just how aroused he is. As I stroke him, his breathing gets faster, a low sound that vibrates against his lips, and I kiss him again.

I pull the rest of my gown away, letting it fall to the floor, and Julian responds by sliding his pants down and guiding me to the bed, our lips never parting for long. With every kiss, I stroke his massive cock.

We collapse onto the bed, his strong arms holding himself over me. He takes each breast into his mouth, his lips and tongue tracing every curve. I shiver and gasp as the sensations ripple through me, my body responding to him. The closeness, the pressure, the way he explores my body with his mouth, overwhelms me, leaving me trembling, caught between anticipation and the ache of need I can't quiet.

A moan escapes my lips as I reach down and slide his cock up and down my slit. Each time his head brushes against my clit, waves of pleasure ripple through my body, and I'm teetering on the edge of ecstasy.

"I love you," he murmurs, his voice low and earnest. "And more than anything, I want to show you how much you mean to me as my mate."

I nod. "Take me, Alpha. I'm yours," I say as I line his cock up with my entrance.

He plunges inside me, and my mouth falls open in a silent gasp as pleasure rips through my body. With each moan, he thrusts harder and faster, and we fall into a perfect rhythm together. "Julian, you feel so good," I gasp.

We move together until rapture builds and floods through us. I hold him close, our bodies tightening and trembling as our climax washes over us, and in that breathless moment, I know there will never be anyone but him.

I love him, too.

17

WORKING AS A TEAM

Julian

I escort Xamara to the breakfast table, and can't bear to take my eyes off her, my beautiful fated mate. The night we spent together has changed something in me. Her touch, her laughter, and the way she looks at me like she understands every part of who I am is so much more than I ever expected. The bond between us is strong, undeniable, and for the first time in perhaps forever, I feel like my life is complete.

I take my place at the head of the table, the morning light dull behind the storm clouds gathering outside. The room feels smaller than usual, crowded with my warriors on one side and Xamara's rogues on the other. Finally, after fighting off the Nighthorn with them twice, I know them by name. I greet them all in turn, and they answer politely. Perhaps we will all be friends.

Last night after we made love, Xamara told me about all of their different talents and abilities. I have a newfound respect for each of them, and I know how we can help one another in the future, when it comes to fighting the coven.

Platters of eggs and fresh bread are passed around the table, everyone eating while the conversation turns to the coven.

"We have new reports," Mason says beside me, his voice low. "Entire herds are missing in Hexeton. A farmstead village burned in Vaeloria. No sign of witches or Nightborn and no tracks."

Nothing left behind. The witches' favorite signature.

"We can't keep losing people," Jax mutters, leaning forward. He braces his hands on the table, his eyes moving over the rogues like he's still weighing whether or not to trust them.

On my other side, Xamara says, "They're hiding their trails behind something. It's like they're using veils."

"They could be casting a spell that's like an invisibility cloak. No one and nothing can see them," Lorna says.

"If you have an idea of how they might be doing this, Lorna, we'll need every detail." I catch her eyes, and she nods.

"They like symmetry. If you disrupt one part, the entire structure collapses." She shrugs and soaks some egg yolk up with a piece of toast.

Kai asks, "What about the vampiric blood in them? We now know they're part vampire."

"That could be important to tracking them," Lark answers. "They're consuming creatures, people, power, anything that strengthens the coven and the new cauldron of Nightborn they undoubtedly created to take out those herds. That's why we're seeing more destruction. They're feeding."

"Lorna, how is your project coming along?" I ask.

"Uh… I mean… it's a work in progress, Your Majesty." She takes a deep breath and doesn't look back at me, which makes me think she still has a long way to go.

Breakfast winds down, but the atmosphere in the dining hall is already charged with anticipation. There's little time for idle chatter now. I rise from my seat at the head of the table, my gaze sweeping over the warriors and rogues gathered around. "We need to stay sharp. I need my warriors, along with you rogues, if you'd like to join us, to head to the training yard. Get your bodies moving, hone your instincts. We're not taking any chances. You've all proven yourselves, but now we need to be better, stronger, and faster. The coven won't wait for us to catch up." I glance at Xamara as I speak, knowing she's already fully aware of what's at stake.

"Lorna," I continue, "I need you and Lark to head to the alchemist tower. There's work to be done, preparing what we'll need for the next phase." I look at Lark. "This is an invitation, not a command. Xamara has told me of your abilities with magic. You're not one of my warriors, but you've earned your place here. If you're willing, I know your knowledge and skills will be invaluable."

She gives me a small smile and a slight nod in response.

Next, I look at the healer. "Willow, if you'd like to, you can go with Helena to the healing center. We'll need both of you supervising as the healers get everything ready for battle."

Again, the acknowledgment is small but positive.

The room stirs with movement as everyone processes my orders; they know the drill. Everyone has a role to play, and none of us can afford to hesitate.

As the warriors and rogues rise to make their way to the training yard, I turn to Xamara. "You," I say, my voice lower now, more private, "stick with me. We'll take a moment to go over the latest reports. Then, we'll check in with everyone."

She looks at me. "I'd love to stick with you." A coy smile turns up the corners of her mouth.

I smirk, shaking my head. "You're going to be trouble, aren't you?" I tap my finger on the report, trying to focus. "They're still operating in the shadows, slipping past our defenses. We need to find their pattern and see if we can anticipate their next strike."

She looks at the report, her eyes narrowed. "I'm pretty good at spotting patterns. Let me take a look."

We spend a few more minutes scanning through the reports, exchanging thoughts, but it's clear that there's little we can act on until we have more information. The coven's methods remain elusive. That's the key to their strategy: stay hidden and confuse the enemy.

When we're done, I gather the reports and rise, motioning for Xamara to follow me. "Let's check on the training. We've got a lot to do, and everyone needs to stay sharp." She slips her hand into mine, and we head down the hall.

Outside, the yard is alive with motion. The warriors and rogues move fluidly, circling one another and testing each other's strength in sparring matches. The rogues are training just as fiercely, showing no sign of hesitation or fear. They've proven themselves time and time again.

I stay in my human form, as does Xamara, watching the wolves with careful discernment. I cross my arms, a sense of pride swelling in my chest. "They're getting better," I murmur. "They're not just training for a fight anymore. They're fighting for their Luna's life."

She looks up at me, her lips parting slightly in question, her eyebrows raised, but before she can speak, an explosion rocks the ground beneath our feet, the deafening sound of shattering glass and cracking stone echoing through the yard. A burst of fire blooms in the distance, lighting up the sky with a sudden, blinding flare. Every wolf in the yard stops, their ears twitching as they look toward the source of the explosion, the heat of the flames reaching us where we stand.

I turn, instinctively reaching for Xamara, just as she jumps into my arms, her heart racing against mine.

I let out a startled laugh, breaking the tension for just a moment. "I've got you."

She looks up at me, her eyes filled with wonder as she surveys the situation. "What the hell was that?"

In the distance, I hear Lorna's voice, though it's muffled by the wind. She's standing in the window of the tower. "We're fine!" she calls, her voice louder now as she waves down to us. "No damage. Just a little... unexpected spark. Lark is fine, too."

I set Xamara down gently, stepping back as we glance back over the training yard. The warriors and rogues continue their intense training, moving with purpose and determination. I know the fight ahead will be fierce, but we'll be ready.

❋

LATER THAT NIGHT, XAMARA AND I SIT AT A SMALL TABLE IN MY chambers, a delicious meal spread before us. The quiet intimacy contrasts sharply with the loud, raucous laughter and clanking dishes from downstairs. The warriors and rogues are still celebrating their progress–and fueling their camaraderie.

"I can't believe how well they're getting along," I remark, glancing toward the door. "It's like they've always been a unit."

My mate nods, smiling. "It's something special, isn't it? They've always had their strengths. The rogues have their independence, and your warriors their discipline. It's as though they needed a common enemy to bring them together." I watch her closely, her expression softening as she speaks, the candles casting light on her gorgeous face.

The sound of the rogues and warriors celebrating below is comforting. It's proof that we're building something strong here. I lean back in my chair, looking out the window as the moonlight spills through the curtains. "My parents used to tell me the world could be a peaceful place, that if we just learned to put aside our differences, we could create a place where everyone is welcome."

She meets my gaze, her eyes searching mine. "You haven't told me much about your family. What happened to your parents?"

I swallow hard, feeling the familiar ache in my chest. "My mother died when I was a young boy. She was sick for years, and no one knew what it was that ailed her. They called it an 'incurable illness,' something that wiped her out slowly. My father spent every moment he could trying to find a cure, but nothing worked. She died when I was six." I pause, swallowing again. "And my father died a few years ago of loneliness. From a broken heart from the severed mate bond. He held on until I was grown. I became Alpha after that."

Xamara's voice softens. "I'm so sorry about your family."

I offer her a small, tight smile. "It's been a long time, but it still hurts. Losing them feels like a lifetime ago, but it still stings."

"I don't know much about my mother," she tells me. "She died when I was a baby. I don't even know what she died from. No one ever speaks of her, so I'm not even certain of her name. My father died just a couple of years ago in battle. That's when Selvara became Luna of Moonfang."

"Selvara," I mutter, the name tasting bitter on my tongue. "She's always been... ambitious."

Xamara's eyes darken, the vulnerability in her expression hardening. "She lied to my father and told him she was a shifter, that she was loyal to the pack, but obviously she's not. She's a witch. A vampiric witch."

Anger rises in my chest again. "The coven has done enough damage, but I promise they won't get to you, Xamara. I swear to you. I will protect you from Selvara and the coven, no matter what it takes."

18

I NEED HIM

Julian and I run side by side, the pack and the rogues fanning out around us, their scents mixing with the sharp tang of the forest. I'm aware of every movement in the underbrush. Our first training drill as one unit is on. When the coven is close again, we have to make sure we're ready.

We've had trackers out looking for them for days, and every time we think we're getting closer, they vanish into the shadows. But that familiar pull of danger and a sense that something is on the move stays with me. We'll find them again soon. I just know it. Every muscle in my body is ready for a fight. We just have to find them. For now, we continue to practice, moving deeper into the trees.

The first drops of rain hit me like a shock of cold fire, startling me from my focus. I barely have time to register the change before the storm breaks. The rain comes in a relentless, punishing torrent, soaking through my fur in seconds. The temperature drops as if the air itself has turned on us. I can't smell anything. Is it possible that the coven sent the storm to throw us off their trail? Surely not.

Visibility drops to near nothing. I can barely see Julian's form ahead of me, just the outline of his dark shape moving in the torrent. The trees, usually so clear, are blurred shadows in the wall of rain.

A roar of thunder cracks so loud it shakes the ground beneath me, and the wind picks up, bending the trees with unnatural force. My fur is slick with ice, but I ignore the cold.

I look at Julian, my heart thrumming in my chest. He's a dark silhouette against the gray sky. I can barely see him running in front of me. The storm is pulling us apart, and the pack is scattering and breaking formation.

"Julian, please don't leave me! The coven could send a new cauldron of Nightborn straight for me!" I call through the mind-link.

I try to dig my claws into the ground, but my paws slip in the mud. I push harder, but the wind howls louder, drowning out everything else.

"I'm just up this ridge. I can see you, and I'm heading back your way," he replies.

I push forward toward the ridge, racing through the dense forest, moving as fast as I can, but it's like the rain is alive, trying to pull my body apart.

The pack scatters, and I can't see any of the rogues through the sheets of rain. Their scents are swallowed by the storm, and every direction I choose feels wrong. I reach out through the mind-link, calling for them, trying to feel their presence, but it's like shouting into a void. No one answers. How can a storm interfere with the mind-link? It can't be magic, can it?

My paws sink into the mud, slowing my pace. *"Keep moving this way!"* Julian's voice flows through my mind. *"I'm right in front of you. We're almost together again."* I trust him completely, letting his certainty guide me through the chaos, letting him pull me closer.

Julian comes into view just ahead of me, making his way back down from the high ground, only a dark shadow before me. I rush forward, my heart pounding in my ears, and finally, I reach him.

"I'll be more careful to stay with you," he assures me.

I nod, and we run together through the storm, the rain hammering against our backs, the forest around us swallowed by a blur of gray. My muscles ache with every stride, the weight of the downpour soaking into my bones, but I keep pace with Julian, moving together, tracking the unseen, listening for the call of danger. The pack is nowhere to be found, the storm throwing them off course.

"Stay close," I hear Julian's voice, pulling me back from the storm's dizzying force. *"We need to find shelter."*

Under our paws, the forest shudders. It's a subtle vibration at first, so faint I almost dismiss it. Then Julian's body stiffens beside me, and the ground pulses again, stronger this time. Trees sway unnaturally as bark rips from their trunks, and mud is sent flying. *"This isn't right,"* I push through the mind-link. *"What if it's the coven?"*

"Let's not get ahead of ourselves," he replies, but the way his eyes move as he looks around us makes me wonder if he thinks I could be right. *"Keep close. Nothing here is ordinary."*

The tremor intensifies, shaking loose wet leaves and sending us sliding across the mud. I press against him instinctively, trusting him to navigate through the instability as rain lashes harder, thunder rolling over us. Every fiber of my being screams that this is dark magic at work, a deliberate disruption, and not a natural storm sent from the Moon Goddess.

Ahead of us, in the side of a hill, a small cave mouth comes into view, half concealed by the trees, offering a temporary refuge. The moment I see it, relief surges through me. My wolf shouts at me to get there, escape the storm, and regroup. *"There's a cave!"* I push harder, Julian close on my heels, the wind battering our bodies.

We reach the cave, and the second we're inside, everything feels different. The roaring storm outside becomes distant, muffled by the thick stone walls. I shake out my fur, water pouring off me in heavy droplets, and Julian does the same. We stand there for a few moments, listening. I hear nothing. Perhaps the coven isn't so close after all.

I keep close to my mate, drawn in ways I can't fully explain. He didn't leave me behind; he waited for me on the ridge, letting me catch up. He's always there when I need him most. That pull toward him, the certainty that he's mine and I'm his, won't let me stay in wolf form any longer. I shift back to my human shape because I need him right now. Despite the storm, the danger, I have to have him–now.

Julian shifts as well, his gaze never leaving me as he slowly stands, his breath heavy. The space between us is charged, and I take a step toward him, my body already aching for him in ways I can't ignore. There's something in his eyes that makes my heart race faster–a need, a promise of something more.

Julian's hand is on my back, pulling me into him. The feel of his body against mine is a shock, the heat of his skin chasing away the lingering chill from the storm. He's strong, and yet, in this moment, there's a tenderness to him that makes me crave him even more. He cups my face, his thumb brushing over my lips.

I raise up on my toes and kiss him. The kiss deepens quickly, the storm outside mirroring the intensity building between us. I press myself closer to him, feeling the hard lines of his body that radiate power. He responds in kind, his hands moving to my waist, pulling me tighter against him.

He reaches around and squeezes my ass, lifting me into the air and pressing me against the stone wall of the cave, his gorgeous brown eyes locked on mine, filled with both love and lust. Holding me up effortlessly with one arm, he uses his other hand to trail his fingers along my slit, leaving me trembling and soaked, craving more.

He kisses me again, and I moan into his mouth. His fingers find my clit, rubbing fast until my legs are shaking, and I'm gasping. When our lips part, I beg him, "Please, Julian. Take me."

Without hesitation, he slides into me, holding my body against the wall with his hands under my thighs, every thrust filling me with ecstasy.

I lift my breasts for him, and he devours them hungrily, sucking and nibbling in a way that sends me over the edge. Waves of pleasure crash over me, and I come again and again, shuddering around him, my body trembling on his cock.

The storm outside can't compete with Julian. The wind and rain feel weak compared to him. His power and intensity are overwhelming, consuming me. Finally, after I've wrung every ounce of energy from my body, riding wave after wave of pleasure, Julian releases inside me, leaving us both spent.

He lifts me gently in his arms, holding me close for a moment before lowering me to the ground inside the cave so I'm standing. The two of us shift back into our wolf forms so we'll be warmer. We cuddle close together and stare out at the opening of the cave as the storm rages on. The ground is cold beneath us, but his body is warm. We lie side by side, our breathing still ragged from what we've shared.

I turn my head to look at him, and he smiles, tired but satisfied. For a while, the storm outside and the world beyond the cave cease to exist, leaving only this quiet, raw closeness, and the certainty that we will face every storm as one.

19

CORRUPTED

The cave is quiet now, the storm has passed, and I snuggle close to Xamara. She's breathtaking, and I can't stop thinking how much she means to me, how good she makes me feel.

"We better go find the others," I say, reluctant to end this moment. But the pack and the rogues will be waiting, and we can't afford to fall behind. I don't think that this storm was created by the coven, but I don't know for certain. If they are nearby, we need to find them.

Xamara nods, determination in her eyes. *"You're right. Let's go."* She rests her paw against mine for a moment before she pulls back, and together, we move to the mouth of the cave, peeking out at the forest, side by side.

It seems that the storm has let up some. Hesitantly, we walk out into the forest. The ground is soft and uneven beneath our paws, with puddles forming and slick leaves sliding underfoot. I push forward, my ears pricked, my senses tuned to the faintest tremor or scent. The rogues and my warriors aren't far—we'll find them.

"Alpha Julian?" Mason's voice comes through the mind-link. *"A group of us followed the storm's path toward Moonfang lands. We believe the*

coven is hiding in the storm. We are all moving toward the border. The rogues are with me.

I growl low. So this was the coven. Part of me wishes I hadn't stopped tracking myself, but Xamara needed me, and at the moment, that was more important. *"We're on our way. Keep everyone together until we arrive."*

"Understood, Alpha," Mason replies.

I glance at Xamara and relay the plan. *"My Beta and a group of warriors are heading toward Moonfang lands. He thinks the coven is causing the storm. We'll meet the others there."*

"Good. Let's move."

The trees blur past as we pick up speed, moving through the woods with the lingering remnants of the storm just ahead of us.

"Do you think the rogues are okay?" she asks, her tone filled with concern.

"They'll be fine," I reply. *"Mason is holding them together, and the pack won't let anything happen to them."*

We round a bend, and the edge of Moonfang territory comes into view. The familiar scent of my pack is sharp and clear in the wet air. A surge of determination pushes me forward.

We meet up with my warriors and the seven rogues in the woods on the border of Moonfang. Xamara runs beside me, matching my pace as we move forward. The forest opens up, the trees giving way to the paths leading into Moonfang's largest village, the storm in front of us obscuring the coven as it moves toward the castle.

Mason's voice cuts through the mind-link, calm and confident. *"Moonfang has always been friendly, an ally, and we've been able to come and go as we please in these pack lands. Do we think that's changed?"*

"You're right. We've been allies before, but with their Luna's true identity revealed, we'll need to be cautious." The last thing I want is to have to fight a pack that we've gotten along with for centuries, but if they attempt to defend the coven, we will have no choice.

A large courtyard opens before us, the soft paths and stone walls usually welcoming, but today, the daylight is swallowed. Above us, the storm lingers, dense and unnatural, a dark canopy that turns afternoon into night.

Thirteen shapes move beneath the false night, walking toward the castle, with Luna Selvara at the center. Years ago, I worked on establishing a peace treaty with her, and even then, she never seemed to be trustworthy.

They slip silently through the castle doors, and we move closer, the pack and rogues together. *"Perfect. We have them trapped,"* I send out to Xamara and all the warriors in my pack.

But something is wrong. The Moonfang warriors, who should be greeting us as allies, stand rigid at the edges of the courtyard.

Their movements are aggressive, their eyes hard and unwelcoming. Then the first growl rips through the tense air. A snap of a jaw, a taut muscle, and suddenly the court erupts into chaos. A pack I trusted, comrades for years, now surge toward us with snarls, their teeth bared, driven by dark magic. My warriors tighten ranks, the rogues fall into formation beside them, and I prepare for a fight we hoped we'd never encounter at these gates.

"Julian," Xamara hisses through the mind-link, *"something's wrong. This isn't like them."*

I growl low in agreement, scanning the pack. The dark magic is thick, twisting loyalty into confusion and rage.

The first lunge comes suddenly. A Moonfang wolf snaps at one of my warriors. I move instantly, intercepting with a powerful push, knocking them off course. The rogues fan out, agile and precise, protecting Xamara and coordinating with my warriors through body language. The attack comes again, then another, each one countered with controlled, deliberate defense.

Xamara moves to flank me, the rogues at her side. Her instincts are sharp, her eyes bright in the storm-streaked light. I send a command through the mind-link, guiding my warriors around her, directing them to neutralize the Moonfang assault without causing permanent harm.

We fight strategically, holding a controlled line, keeping Xamara safe at the center. My focus narrows, every movement deliberate, every growl and motion a warning or command. The coven's magic hums in the background, a darkness twisting the once-friendly pack, but we are precise, disciplined, and unyielding.

Breathing hard, I keep my eyes on Xamara. Even surrounded by aggression, she remains the center, the reason, the fated mate who drives my every move. We will protect each other, and we will survive this.

"Protect Xamara. The coven wants her blood." I call through the mind-link. My warriors fan out around her, the rogues weaving through the attackers, each move precise. Havelock cuts off one charging wolf. Seamus flips around another, nimble and teasing the enemy without leaving an opening. Mac drives one back with sheer force, while Willow darts between blows. Ivy draws their attention, taunting and drawing strikes away from Xamara. Lark moves like liquid, ripping through their flank and cutting off the momentum of the attack. And Ian never leaves Xamara's side.

"They have been corrupted by the witches to attack. They want Xamara's blood, but we won't let them near her."

The Moonfang wolves snap and lunge with a focus that makes my blood boil. They're after her. Every time one lunges too close, I intercept, my jaws clamping and claws striking, keeping her out of reach. My warriors mirror my moves, forming a coordinated wall of protection that bends but never breaks.

One wolf slides beneath the line. His teeth are aimed at Xamara, but I move faster, pinning him back with a sweep of my paws. Mason covers the left, Jax the right, with Simeon and Kai forming the center with Zara.

Above us, the false night covers the witches, who move like predators cloaked in storm. Luna Selvara's presence is unmistakable, radiating control, feeding their frenzy. I won't let my mate be touched. We will protect Xamara.

I lunge forward, snapping at an attacker and sending him skidding back. Xamara is right beside me, holding her own, striking when she can, moving with instinct and determination.

The Moonfang wolves close in around us, their teeth flashing. I counter every strike, predict their rhythm, anticipate the magic that guides them. We know who they want.

"Stay close to her," I order. Xamara ducks and weaves, just far enough to avoid claws, just close enough that I can intercept.

When a Moonfang wolf lunges for her side again, I lunge. My jaws close around its throat. I shake it and toss it to the side. We form a wall that can't be breached. Through it all, I think only of Xamara's life, safety, and the mate bond that makes me fight harder than I've ever fought before.

This ends now. This ends with her alive. We will break them here and now beneath the shadow of Selvara's dark sky. No one touches Xamara. Not while I breathe. Not while I fight.

2 0

LOYALTY AND COMPASSION

I skid to a halt, and my claws bite into the frozen earth. My breathing is sharp and ragged. The Moonfang battlefield stretches before me like a living nightmare, wolves snarling and blood darkening the snow. My chest tightens, my instincts screaming, but it isn't fear that freezes me. It's the scent of my people, my friends, in the midst of chaos meant to tear us all apart.

"No. No. This isn't right!" I shout through the mind-link.

Julian's warriors and my rogues are being attacked by members of my pack. My heart pounds as I realize what this means: friends on both sides could die today because of a battle I never wanted. Honestly, none of us want this. Only the coven. I grit my teeth, flex my claws, and focus. Loyalty demands action. Compassion demands restraint.

I reach for Julian in the mind-link. *"Pull back! Pull your warriors back! Please stop! Now!"*

I feel his hesitation, but there's no room for doubt. I hammer the command again, firmer this time, and the pulse of his response shifts. The tension eases. His warriors pause, faltering mid-attack, as if they've received the sudden change in orders.

Then I reach out to the rogues. *"Disengage. Retreat with me. We leave now, quickly and carefully. Cover each other. We stay together."*

I lead them in a swift retreat, moving away from the battlefield as fast as we can. Every step carries the urgency of escape, every glance toward the enemy a silent plea that they don't follow. Soon enough, we reach the Moonfang border, and finally, relief washes over me when we see the enemy has not pursued us past the territory line.

We surge through the trees, paws slipping on the uneven ground. The rogues are tense around me. Their ears are pinned back. Low growls vibrate in the air. They are angry, frustrated, even with the fight over, and it's clear it's directed at me. I called the retreat.

"Xamara, why pull us back?" Seamus snaps. His muscles are tense as if he's ready to spin back into the fight.

"Those are my people, and they didn't even know they were fighting. They are under the coven's spell. It wouldn't be right to fight them against their will."

Havelock's voice is sharp. *"I know you're right, but it still stings. We wanted to finish it."*

"I understand. I wish it was over, too, but not like that." I meet their gazes one by one, and they nod in understanding.

Finally, we cross into Blackwater territory. Some members of our pack were wounded in our fight, but no one was killed. Still, I shiver at how easily the battle could have turned fatal. For now, we need to keep moving, put distance between the two sides, and come up with a new strategy now that we know the coven has control of the warriors.

The forest finally gives way to the familiar hills overlooking Julian's castle. I pause at the edge of the woods. My nose twitches while I take in the scents of familiarity–of safety–after the black magic we just faced.

When we reach the castle gate, Julian is at the head of the group, many of his warriors right behind him. I hang back. He turns and looks at me, and I give him a reassuring smile. He nods and continues at the front. I continue to keep my distance when we enter the courtyard. Servants and guards hurriedly open gates and doors for us, guiding us through the castle entrance so we don't have to shift. Once inside, I slip toward my chamber, keeping to the shadows, and wait until I am alone before shifting back into human form.

I dress quickly, taking a few moments to breathe and calm myself down before stepping back out into the hall. A moment later, Julian calls a meeting through the mind-link. He's already seated, along with his leaders, when I reach the war room. I notice that the rogues aren't here yet, but surely, they'll be here soon.

Julian is pacing. Some of his warriors are frowning in my direction. Mason's eyes are blazing.

"You pulled us back?" the Beta snaps at me. "After everything we've done? After they tried to kill you?"

I meet his eyes. "Yes, I pulled us back," I say firmly. Julian steps over, but I put my hand on his arm to stop him. I can handle this. "Because those wolves, those *people*, are my pack. They're my family. I will not spill their blood, even if they are being manipulated by my stepmother's magic. I can't, and I won't, cross that line."

A ripple of murmurs runs through the room. Some of the warriors still look furious with me.

Julian's voice is tight. "They're under dark magic. It wasn't their fault."

Mason opens his mouth, closes it, and looks away before saying, "We could end the threat now, once and for all. Why hold back?"

"Moonfang Pack isn't the enemy. The coven is the enemy, and they'll only use more Nightborn or another pack to fight us until they have my blood," I explain, looking at everyone, not just the man who asked the question. "Killing my pack members will do no good. Ending the temporary threat at the cost of innocent lives makes *us* no better than the enemy. I fight for survival, yes, but not at the cost of my people. I would die for them."

For a long moment, the room is still. Julian stands next to me, the resolve in his stance mirroring mine, and the moral clarity I wear like armor.

Mason hesitates, clearly wrestling with the truth he can't dismiss.

Loyalty, integrity, and family are all more important than a simple victory.

"You're right," Mason finally admits. "I apologize."

"I understand." I mean it. It's easy to see where he's coming from. "Even if it costs us advantage, resources, or time, we have to do what's right. Even if it costs me my life. I won't let innocent blood be shed. Moonfang and Blackwater should remain allies."

"You're not just a warrior," Julian mutters, moving closer to me. "You think like a leader. Strategy meets ethics. You hold the lines that others cross too easily."

The argument simmers, and gradually, an understanding takes shape. Julian exhales slowly and turns to his warriors. "We will adapt," he says. "Xamara is correct. We can't lose ourselves, our values, *especially* in the midst of war. That's why I initially gave the order to only wound and not kill, but she was right to call the retreat."

I nod, relieved, but I keep my guard up. The war is far from over. Still, for now, tension eases.

We begin to outline the next steps. Julian's leaders give recommendations with firm voices and focused minds. The room is heavy with purpose, and I know, even in the heat of frustration and fear, that we are stronger for the restraint we exercised, for the morality we upheld.

"We can't confront them directly," I remind everyone. "We've tried that more than once, and it never works. What we must do is turn their magic against them. They rely on their spells, and the way they use the weather to move directly in front of us shows that they are overly confident. They use curses, enchantments, and illusions to dominate and control everything and everyone around them. However, if we can manipulate the battlefield, the environment, and their expectations, we can make their magic work *for* us, not against us."

Mason adds, "We know their patterns. We can predict their maneuvers. Their arrogance is a weapon if we bait it correctly."

"Exactly, " I say, feeling a surge of hope.

That's when I glance around the war room and freeze. The rogues still aren't here. Normally, they would be. Panic coils in my chest. "Wait—where are the rogues?" I demand, my voice frantic. "Has anyone seen them?"

"No," one of the warriors answers, shaking his head. "They came back with us, but they haven't joined us yet."

I reach for them in the link. *"Are you here? We need you in the war room."*

There's a hollow, oppressive silence. My stomach churns. Something is definitely wrong.

I try again, this time more urgently. *"Hello? Please respond!"*

Still nothing. My mind races through every possibility. Are they scouting the borders? Were they ambushed? Did they go back to Moonfang? Are they trapped?

Julian notices the change in my expression. "Xamara?" His voice carries an edge of concern.

"My friends aren't here," I repeat, shaking my head. "I can't reach them through the mind-link. They must've gone back to the fight."

"Don't worry, Xamara. We'll find them."

He turns to his Mason. "Take a patrol. Search the perimeter, the forest, and every likely path. Bring the rogues back safely."

I swallow, biting back the urgent need to bolt after them. "I want to go," I say. "I should go with them. I can find them through the mind-link."

"No." Julian cuts me off firmly. "You stay here. It's too dangerous for you to go back. This patrol is already high risk."

Panic flares hotter in my chest. "But they're my friends! I need to—"

"Xamara," Julian's tone softens slightly, but the authority is still there. "I won't argue about this with you. The coven wants you dead. You stay here. That's an order."

I grit my teeth, reluctantly falling silent, though my eyes begin to water as I fight back tears. Mason and a group of warriors leave to search for the rogues. We try to continue the conversation about our plans, but without knowing what's happening, it's pointless. Minutes crawl by, each one stretching endlessly. Finally, Julian sighs and says, "We need to go to the lookout tower."

"Why?" I ask, going along with him.

He takes my hand and leads me toward the tower. "We'll be above the forest. Maybe we can spot them. Maybe we can help narrow the search."

I walk with him up the stairs. Wind blows through the arrow slots, whipping at my hair as we climb. At the top, I look through the telescope and scan the forest, the cliffs, every shadow and tree line. Nothing. A cold, sinking dread rolls over me.

"They're out there," I whisper, trying to calm myself down. "And I feel like something isn't right. I need to join the patrol."

Julian glances at me sideways. "No way. The witches will send the Nightborn after you."

I grit my teeth, scanning the forest again. My friends are in danger. I feel it! And every second they remain missing feels like an eternity.

"I have to go," I insist. "They're my pack. They've saved my life more than once. I need to be with them."

His jaw tightens, and he steps closer. "Xamara, you just called a retreat. The rogues don't listen to anybody, and they're out there being reckless."

"But I'm the only one who can reach them through the mind-link!" I snap. "Mason and the others can't speak to them or locate them with anything but scent."

"If we go out there, you stay next to me. Every step. No exceptions."

"Agreed. I won't leave your side."

"Then we move together?"

I nod. "Let's go," I whisper.

He gives me one last side-eyed glance before nodding. We move down the tower steps in a rush. My every thought is on the rogues.

At the edge of the clearing, we shift, bones and fur forming, claws appearing. In wolf form, side by side, we race into the forest to join the patrol and search for the rogues.

21

RIP HER APART

*

Julian*

The forest deepens around us, dark and dense. Branches snag our fur as Xamara and I sprint toward the Gleabhain River. I can smell the fight before I see it: blood, fear, and churned earth, all of it sharp in the cold air. The clash of bodies carries through the trees in violent echoes. My warriors are engaged with something, snarling and striking with full force, though I still can't tell who or what they are facing. All I know is that it is powerful, and the situation is escalating fast. I tell them we're coming, angling toward the sound, ready to break into the fight, but Mason's voice cuts through the mind-link before I can take another step.

"Alpha, don't come this way," he says firmly *"We've got this fight covered, and we don't want the Nightborn seeing Xamara. Keep her safe. Just focus on finding the rogues."*

I grit my teeth, but Mason is right. My warriors will fight well, and Xamara's safety comes first. I look at her, and she meets my eyes, trust and urgency mirrored there. *"This way!"*

We change direction, moving quickly but cautiously through the underbrush, letting the shadows hide us as best they can.

Tracking the rogues isn't easy. The forest is alive with scents and sounds, every rustle a potential threat. I reach for Xamara through the mind-link. *"Anything from them?"*

"No. Nothing."

We run even deeper into the woods, and then I pick up the familiar odor of the rogues cutting through the pine and snow. I reach Xamara through the mid-link. *"There. That's them,"* I whisper.

She freezes instantly, lifting her nose. We follow the trail until the trees open into a small clearing. The seven rogues have Luna Selvara cornered. She trembles violently, crying out, terror written across her face as the wolves close in around her. Growls fill the night air.

They move with precise coordination, closing around Luna Selvara. She struggles against them, her hands trembling as she tries to unleash her magic, but Lark steps forward. A shimmering veil of violet and soft lavender unfurls from her, twisting and curling through the air, forming an enchanted barrier that halts Selvara's spells before they can take shape. Each flicker of energy that Luna Selvara forces into being is swallowed by the ward, leaving her powerless and terrified. The rogues hold her firmly, their eyes unflinching and bodies tense, leaving no room for escape or resistance.

"No, this can't be! Release me! I will not be powerless!" she screams as she forces spell after spell, but Lark's magic contains her effortlessly, keeping her under control.

Stunned, I stand there for a moment, gawking. I had no idea Lark had powers. I look at Xamara, but all she can do is shrug.

Seamus and Willow press Luna Selvara to the ground, holding her arms and legs with unyielding strength, their weight keeping her from rising. She thrashes, screaming in frustration and fury, but the rogues are precise, their movements practiced and synchronized. Havelock steps forward, a rope hung loosely around his neck. He tosses it with a flip of his head and catches it in his jaws. Then he throws it over the witch, cinching it tight. Selvara struggles against the bindings, but the rogues' grip is absolute, and she can do nothing but wriggle beneath them.

With his head tucked under her torso, Havelock heaves her onto his back. His teeth clamp down on the rope around her. Selvara's magic flares violently, trying to lash out, but Lark's enchantment surges. A shimmering barrier of energy drains the power from her spells until they fizzle into nothing.

We move swiftly through the forest, Havelock carrying Selvara, the rest of the rogues flanking us, until the scent of the castle rises ahead. I have so many questions. How did they catch her? Where are the other witches? Since when does Lark have such strong powers?

The trees thin when we reach the courtyard. Xamara's presence beside me is unwavering, and I can't help the surge of gratitude and pride in the rogues that runs through me. They found the leader of the coven and neutralized at least one of the threats.

The guards throw open the castle doors, and we slip inside. Havelock drops Selvara in the main hall with a solid thud. Immediately, the group tightens around her, showing their teeth. Rage boils in each of us, and we all want to rip her apart.

"Don't let them kill her yet. We need the rest of the coven," I say to Xamara through the mind-link. She relays my message, and the rogues freeze. Their bodies lower, but they keep Selvara contained.

"We need to shift. Tell them we'll return here once we're ready," I say through the mind-link.

"Understood," Xamara replies, her voice sharp and controlled. We slip back from the hall, moving quickly.

When Xamara and I return in human form, fully clothed, the rogues remain in position, circling Selvara.

I speak firmly to the guards, two of the largest men in the castle. "Take her to a cell in the dungeon. Secure her wrists and ankles, and make sure she's locked in tight."

Next, I tilt my head toward the rogues. "Go shift, dress, and meet us in the war room," I tell them firmly. "Do not run off to chase the other witches. We need you whole, focused, and together."

The rogues head toward their chambers, and just then, I hear Mason through the mind-link. *"Alpha, we're on our way back. We defeated the cauldron of Nightborn but lost the rest of the coven."*

"Understood. Don't worry about the rest of the coven for now. Bring

everyone home safely. We have the Luna," I reply. *"And Mason, meet us in the war room. We'll discuss next steps then."*

Once in the war room, I gather my leaders, Xamara, and the rogues. We stand together, ready to decide what to do with Luna Selvara. Xamara meets my eyes, her anger clear, and the rogues remain close, alert and waiting for instructions.

Xamara looks at the rogue. "Why in the hell did you go back out there without me?" she asks, her voice filled with hurt and dismay.

"Your blood draws the Nightborn and the witches," Ivy says. "We couldn't keep watching them attack you. We've been terrified they'll hurt you, and we care too much for you to let that happen."

Voices rise and fall, some calling for Selvara's immediate execution, others urging caution. The coven can't be given leverage. One of my warriors slams a fist against the table. "We should make her pay now! She tried to kill us!"

"I understand," I say firmly. "But we must think rationally. If we kill her now, we'll lose track of the other twelve witches."

The room quiets as Xamara steps forward. "She's my stepmother," she says. "I know her better than any of you. She's cruel, evil, and she never loved me, but she still wants to survive, and that is the one thing she has always cared about. If I speak to her, she may trade preserving her life for the locations of the other twelve witches. When we have that information, we can trap every one of them."

Silence settles over the room as the warriors and rogues exchange looks.

"We'll start there," I reply. "That's our first move. While she speaks with Selvara, the warriors, rogues, and I will lay plans for the other twelve."

Mac steps forward. "We captured Selvara as she was moving through the woods heading up into the Montelune Mountains. Undoubtedly, that's where the rest of the coven hides."

"It was easier to capture her on her own—but still quite difficult,," Lark adds. "The other twelve witches won't be easy either. They'll be hidden in the caves, and will use magic against us. We need a plan— and a good one."

The room falls quiet with the intensity of the plan. In the dungeon, Luna Selvara waits, trapped and powerless, unaware of what she will be forced to reveal.

We begin assembling the threads of our next move, every mind in the room aligned on the same goal: the other twelve witches will not escape. For now, the coven's shadow looms, but the first pieces are in place, and the game has only just begun.

22

ULTIMATUM

I stand in the cold dungeon cell, the damp air suffocating as I take in the woman chained to the far wall. Selvara's iron cuffs glow faintly where her magic strains and sputters beneath them, but the rest of her is a shadow of the creature she once pretended to be.

She's a far cry from the woman she used to be, seated on Moonfang's throne, draped in silk and stolen authority, holding herself with the poised confidence of someone who believed she deserved a crown. She moved among the pack as if she belonged, mimicking the strength of a shifter.

But here in the dim light, her hair hangs in tangled ropes over her shoulders, and her skin looks colorless and papery, stretched too thin over her bones. The illusion she built, brick by brick, has crumbled completely. Without her stolen glamour, she appears smaller, weaker, and brittle. The truth has finally begun to devour her from the inside out. Only her eyes remain unchanged, filled with malice and hunger, an indication that she's still refusing to admit how far she has fallen.

I remind myself that she can't hurt me like this. The spell-forged cuffs clamp her wrists and ankles, the runes carved into the metal suppressing every ounce of her magic. She's bound and contained, held fast so completely that she is no threat at all. Even now, as she strains against the chains, I can see the effort wasted in powerless gestures.

Yet, when she lifts her head and smiles, my chest tightens, and I clench my hands. I remember when I was a little girl, she always pretended to be kind in front of others, especially in front of my father.

But behind closed doors, her words cut, and her punishments were cruel. The fear she planted in me then strangles my lungs even now. Even chained and weakened, she can still make me feel small.

"So the little heir thinks she's won." Her voice drips through the dungeon like poison, coating every stone. "Moonfang and Blackwater playing at freedom. Your precious wolves believe they're safe."

I don't answer. I won't give her the satisfaction.

Her smile widens. "But safety comes at a cost, Xamara. That is what you refuse to learn."

A pulse of cold sweeps through the room, sharp and biting, curling around me with a pressure that feels almost alive, as if invisible fingers are gripping my chest and twisting my heart. The sensation is new, and it carries a power that makes my spine tingle and my heart pound. It's a dark force that could bend an entire pack into obedience if it were unleashed. Even now, weakened and chained, Selvara's presence presses through the space between us, relentless and undeniable, and I feel it crawling along my skin, whispering of black magic.

"You feel it, don't you?" she asks. "The black spirits want to rise again. They always answer to me."

"I'm not here to talk about your evil power." My voice comes out hard, calmer than I feel. "I'm here for answers."

She rolls her shoulders as much as the chains allow, as if settling into a throne instead of a filthy floor. "Then I'll give you an ultimatum. You've always hated ultimatums, haven't you? Either you allow me to remain in power, and let my coven keep their hold over Moonfang, or you will die."

The words fall like an axe between us.

"That's your offer?" I ask.

"That is your salvation."

"You think I'm afraid of you, Selvara?"

"You should be. I may be reduced, but I am never without my dark power, and neither are the witches who follow me."

The cold pulse drags along my spine again, rolling through my muscles and sliding under my skin like ice-laced fingers, and my claws pop out as a reflex, sharp and aching against my palms. But I don't shift. I don't move because I know she can't hurt me.

I take one step closer, then another, until she has to tilt her chin up to meet my eyes.

"It's my turn now," I say. "You're going to tell me where the rest of the coven is hiding."

"And why," she sneers, "would I ever—"

"Because if you don't," I cut in, "I'll walk out of this cell, call the guards, and let them kill you where you sit."

For the first time, her smile falters.

Chains rattle as she straightens, her movements jerking with the tension of a wounded animal struggling against its restraints. "You wouldn't dare. Xamara, I'm your stepmother."

"I would," I say, harsh and cold. "And you know you'd deserve it. You lied to my father, pretended to be one of us, pretended to be a shifter, just so you could marry him and claim the throne that should have been mine. You made the Nightborn ravage Vaeloria and Hexeton, destroy entire lands, attack my friends and my mate's pack, all to increase your power. I figured out every scheme, every manipulation, every cruel step you took to get what you wanted, and now you're nothing more than a beaten-down, desperate shadow of yourself, struggling uselessly against chains you can't break."

She gasps.

I lean in just a fraction, enough for her to feel the truth in my voice. "Tell me where they are, Selvara. This is the only mercy you're getting."

For a long moment, she just stares at me, her eyes stoic, with a trace of fear behind her pupils. The smile she used to wear like a mask melts away. The venom, the carefully measured cruelty, all of it slowly vanishes, leaving only the tremor of a woman who finally realizes that her time is up, that the power she clung to with every lie and threat has slipped through her fingers, and for the first time, she looks small, exposed, and undeniably mortal.

I don't wait. I step back, lift my chin toward the iron door, and call, "Guards!"

The scrape of boots on stone echoes down the corridor. Selvara's eyes move toward the sound.

Two guards enter, waiting for my command.

I fold my arms. "Selvara, this is your last chance."

The witch inhales sharply, and it comes out as a quiet hiss, a whisper of surrender edged with anger and disbelief. "Fine," she snaps. "You want to know where the coven hides? They're in the Montelune Mountains just east of the Gleabhain River." Her lip curls in a mocking smile. "But I promise you, my coven and the Nightborn can protect themselves against any pack."

I push the information through the mind-link immediately. *"Julian, the coven is hiding in the Montelune Mountains. They're in the caves just east of the Gleabhain River."*

"Good work, Xamara. Please stay in the castle. Get out of the dungeon. Do not leave until I get back. I've asked Ian to stay with you, and the rest of us are going to bring the coven in."

I take a step toward the doorway when a harsh, rattling laugh cuts through the cell. I whirl around just in time to see every iron cuff flare red with violent light.

"No—" I stumble back as the chains explode with a burst of black magic. Iron shatters across the floor. Selvara stands, her wrists raw, and her ankles bleeding. Her eyes burn with a manic, triumphant light.

Before the guards can react, she lifts both hands and begins to chant.

Her voice winds through the dungeon, rough and urgent, tugging at my chest and throat as if it wants to force me forward. My muscles tighten, my heart jerks in my ribcage, and something hooks inside me, sharp and insistent, pulling at me as a wave of pain hits like a blade driven into bone.

I choke, collapsing to one knee as fire rips through every vein. My muscles seize. My lungs crush inward. The spell claws for my soul, trying to bind me, break me, and hollow me out.

"Xamara," Selvara croons, her voice echoing, splitting, swelling with power. "You should have accepted my offer."

A scream tears from my throat, raw and strangled, and before I can think, a roar fills the dungeon. Silver fur streaks past, teeth flashing, and Ian crashes into Selvara with unstoppable force, hurling her across the stone floor. She hits hard, and for a moment, she glares at him, disbelief and rage burning in her eyes, but she doesn't stop chanting.

He launches himself at Selvara again, crashing into her chest and breaking her chant. The spell snaps, the pain stops, and I collapse, shaking and gasping for air.

The witch snarls, twisting her body with sudden, wild force, and hurls her hand toward me. Her voice snaps the edges of the incantation like a whip. Black magic tears through the room, dense and suffocating, writhing with a lethal intent that makes my stomach lurch and every instinct scream of danger before I can even think of a plan. Dark shapes, like twisted shadows with gleaming eyes, swirl in the air around her, writhing and pulsing as if alive, and I can't look away, caught between terror and shock at the horror she has unleashed that's headed directly toward me again.

Then, a flash of silver fur darts in front of me, just as the shadows are about to coil around me again.

"Ian—NO!"

Ian doesn't listen. He stands firm out of sheer bravery, holding his ground between me and the shadows, until the darkness hits him full force. His body jerks violently, thrashing once in a burst of agony, and then he collapses, silver fur paling, dimming, fading as if life itself is being ripped from his body.

"That was meant for you!" Selvara screams. "It would have made me stronger if it had hit you, not that fucking mangy rogue!"

The spell that should have struck me lashes out at Ian instead, and now he's trembling, the tremendous pain I was in only moments ago eating at his insides. Selvara collapses to the floor, unconscious, her magic spent, and her body limp.

"Ian…" My voice breaks. I crawl to him. My hands are trembling so hard I can barely touch him. "Ian, please—no—please don't die!"

The guards from before begin moving again, now that the spell has dissipated, shouting, telling me to stay back. They swarm Selvara, chaining her again, tightening the cuffs, adding additional binding.

All I can do is hold Ian's still body against mine–and scream.

2 3

REVENGE

Xᴀᴍᴀʀᴀ

Ian's silver wolf lies in my lap on the cold dungeon floor, completely still. My stomach churns as I stare at him helplessly. I have to do something. I have to get help.

I reach for Julian through the mind-link, my thoughts a raw and ragged blur. *"Julian, Ian's hurt! He's been hit by Selvara's spell. He's not moving, and I think he's gone. I need help. Please, send Willow back. I can't handle this alone!"*

Julian replies almost immediately. *"I'm sending Willow. Xamara, you need to take Ian to Apothecary Hollow right now. Tell the guards to carry him there. Helena will do everything she can."*

I swallow hard against the lump in my throat and force myself to speak clearly to the guards. "Two of you, carry him to the healing center." The guards comply, lifting Ian between them, and I follow close enough to guide their path, ignoring the jolts of leftover pain from the spell that shoot through my body with every step.

I glance back at Selvara, lying sprawled on the floor, utterly drained, unconscious, her magic completely gone. More guards remain stationed around her, keeping watch, though she can no longer move or threaten anyone. I force myself not to look at her too long, the fury and terror she unleashed still burning in my chest, and focus on getting Ian to help.

The dungeon fades behind me as the guards carry Ian through the corridors. My friend lies motionless, his silver fur dulled, his body limp and unresponsive. My stomach knots, and I can't stop the tears. Ian risked everything to save me, and now he's gone....

We reach the healing center, and the guards place Ian carefully on the table. Healers move quickly around him, gathering herbs and preparing their spells, every motion purposeful. Julian must have used the mind-link to alert Helena ahead of time. Everyone is in motion, coordinated, and ready to try to save him. I stay close, with trembling hands, staring at his still, silent form, helpless but aware that the healers will do whatever they can.

"Helena! Help him!" My voice cracks, raw and desperate. "He's been hit by the witch's dark spell. Please, you have to save him!"

Helena and the other healers hover over Ian. Their hands move quickly even as worry flashes across their faces when they realize there's no pulse, and he's not breathing. Fear fills their eyes, but they don't stop. They work frantically, calling out instructions, weaving spells, and trying everything they can to bring him back.

"Ian, please," I whisper. My voice breaks. "Stay with us. You can't leave me. Please." The words spill out uncontrollably, each one laced with panic and grief. I press my face into my hands and cry.

Maybe thirty minutes into Helena's work, the doors swing open, and Willow flies in, her red hair falling across her pale face, blue eyes wide at the sight of Ian. Tears streak her cheeks, but she moves immediately to his side, joining Helena as their hands weave magic over him.

I can't do anything but stay near, whispering and sobbing. "Help him! Please! He saved me! He can't die!" My cries echo off the walls, desperate and broken, but I can only watch, powerless.

Willow and Helena's hands glow faintly as they work. Energy weaves through the room. I see the magic glow and flicker over Ian's lifeless body and feel the tension around me increasing. My body shakes with sorrow, my legs threatening to give out.

I crouch, pressing my hands to my face, sobs wracking me. Every instinct screams at me to do more, to move, to somehow make him wake up, but I can't. All I can do is watch the healers work to bring him back.

I keep repeating his name, my voice rough and ragged. "Please… don't leave us. Please, Ian…" Each word is a prayer to the Moon Goddess, a plea, a desperate insistence that the friend who risked his life for me may live.

After a few moments, I realize I'm doing nothing to help anyone at the moment. I take a deep breath, wipe my eyes, and pull myself together. On unsteady feet, I approach the table. "Willow, how far into the forest did Julian make it?"

Willow lifts her red-rimmed eyes. "We hadn't made it too far. Such a large group can't move too quickly. Maybe… ten, fifteen miles? Julian had his alchemist, Lorna, use a spell to enhance the mind-link, so we can all speak to each other in our wolf forms. I was toward the back of the pack, so I was able to get here quickly when he told me to turn around."

I nod, bitter sadness mingling with resolve. "Stay here with him. Keep trying to save him. Anything you can think might help, try it."

She swallows and nods, tears pouring down her face, but she doesn't stop, carefully preparing potions and arranging herbs, all in an effort to help poor Ian.

My muscles tremble from exhaustion and the lingering effects of Selvara's attack, but my decision is made. "I'm going to join Julian in battle," I say.

Willow raises an eyebrow, but doesn't argue. With a slight nod, her hands still glowing faintly over Ian's unmoving body, she whispers, "Go. Do what you have to. We'll keep trying here."

Stealing one last look at Ian, I turn and walk away, knowing there's nothing I can do for him here, but I can make sure the Nightborn and the coven pay for what they've done. The forest calls, the battle waits, and I have to be there to see it through.

The moment I reach the outer courtyard, I shed the last hesitation, letting the melancholy sharpen into a single focus. My clothes tear, stretching and ripping against my changing body as I shift. With a speed I've never channeled before, I bolt toward the castle gates, driven by vehemence and revenge. The castle recedes behind me, its walls and towers shrinking in the distance, and all that matters is the path ahead.

The forest darkens around me, shadows stretching longer as the sun sinks, and the cold bite of winter seeps through my fur, stiffening my muscles and making every branch and frozen leaf snap underfoot. I don't slow, letting my legs carry me faster, my senses straining to catch every scent and sound. I reach for my mate through the mind-link. *"Julian, where are you?"*

Silence answers me as I push again, harder, imagining his form running through the trees, and still nothing. I tell myself he can't be too far away. The link fades with distance, but he can't be that far ahead of me based on what Willow said. I curse against the frustration, forcing myself to run faster. Maybe he's too busy to respond.

The Gleabhain River comes into view, its water churning black. I plunge in. Claws scrape stone. Icy water bites at my pelt, and I fight the current. My legs thrash, and my muscles strain until I drag myself onto the far bank. The cold clings, but I shake it off. Though my lungs are burning, my nostrils are flaring, so I immediately catch a faint, unmistakable trace of Julian, just distinct enough to follow. Filled with a mix of relief and urgency, woe from the losses I've endured fuels my drive forward.

Through the snowy path of tangled roots, I follow them, the scent growing stronger with each step. Twilight dims further, the trees massive and looming, but I don't slow down. I weave through the thickening gloom with my ears alert to every sound. I pause briefly, reaching out again. *"Julian, I'm almost there. I can scent your trail!"*

This time I get a response. *"Xamara! Are you all right?"*

Relief, raw and immediate, flows through me at his words. *"I'm fine. I came to fight on Ian's behalf. This dark magic took him from us, and now we will take everything from the coven."*

"Hurry!" he urges. *"We'll wait for you at the base of the mountains."*

Powered on by his urgency, I run on, and soon enough, I emerge from the last tangle of brush into a small clearing just below the lower slopes of the Montelune Mountains, their peaks dark against the fading sunset.

Julian stands at the center, coal-black warriors around him, and the five rogues flank them. *"Xamara!"* I hear the relief in his voice and run to him.

The five rogues all look at me, and I catch their eyes, seeing both pain and acknowledgment that they're glad I'm here. I hope they know how truly sorry I am about Ian, but that will have to wait for another day. I rush to Julian and press my nose into his neck.

For a moment, no one moves. The cold wind sweeps through the clearing, carrying the bitter sting of winter and everything I've lost. Julian looks into my eyes, understanding passing between us without a word. I step forward. Mourning and indignation tighten into something fierce and unbreakable inside me. Whatever waits on that mountain, whatever darkness the coven has left to throw at us, we will face it together now–and we will not turn back this time until this battle is over.

2 4

HORROR AND HOPE

JULIAN

The wind cuts across the Montelune slopes, icy and unrelenting, whipping against our fur and sending shivers through me. Twilight bleeds into night, and the snow beneath our paws is so cold that they have grown numb. Xamara runs beside me, her beautiful white coat a stark contrast against the dark shapes of my wolves.

Lark and Lorna stay close, satchels secured across their backs, moving with the rest of the pack in silent, practiced formation.

I lift my nose, drawing the air in, tracing every scent the wind carries. Eventually, I catch the smell of dark magic almost buried beneath the pine.

I reach out to the pack through the mind-link. *"They're close. Stay sharp."* Mason and Simeon mirror my movements on one side; Jax, Zara, and Kai move in tandem on the other, scanning the shadows. Every sense is stretched to catch even the slightest trace of Nightborn.

The remaining rogues that are joining us spread along the flanks, keeping pace without slowing the pack. Havelock pads steadily beside Lark, her lavender fur brushing against her satchel strap. Seamus, Mac, and Ivy track slightly ahead, sniffing and listening, their move-

153

ments fluid and deliberate. I can feel the tension in the group; the air is filled with anticipation, each of us aware that the coven waits somewhere in these peaks.

Branches snap under our claws, and the thick layer of snow crunches with every step. The mountains rise steep and unforgiving, jagged ridges cutting dark shapes into the dimming sky. My breath fogs in front of me, and my chest burns with exertion, but I push forward, all my senses straining. Xamara darts briefly ahead, scenting, testing the wind, then falls back, staying close. Even in wolf form, she radiates courage.

A faint trace of herbs, smoke, and something unholy drifts to me. I signal through the mind-link for the pack to tighten their formation.

Lorna stays in the center. The others move silently, careful with their footing on the rocky, snow-streaked ridge. They check every shadow and listen for any unnatural movement.

Night swallows day, the mountains eating what little light remains. I focus on the scents, letting them guide me. Xamara's thought reaches me through the mind-link. *"Careful. We're almost there,"* she warns, relief and tension entwined in her words.

A gust of wind carries the unmistakable tang of dark power down from the peaks above. Every wolf stiffens, our tails lowering, and our ears swiveling. My pack, Xamara, the rogues––we're all ready. We move forward together, silent and lethal, closer to the Montelune heights where the witch coven waits, unaware that we are hunting them.

Finally, we see their lair. The cave yawns before us like a black wound in the mountainside, its mouth edged with frost, and the scent of decay and rot curls faintly from within.

We crouch low on the ridge, Xamara beside me, our shapes swallowed by shadows. Lorna and Lark slip behind a cluster of pines and snow-draped brush. I can't see their forms, but I know they're using magic and skill.

When Lorna and Lark emerge, they are no longer wolves. Lorna is clad in black from head to toe, the fabric absorbing what little light clings to the mountainside. Lark stands in lavender, the soft fabric draping over her lithe frame, catching the moonlight. Her skin is a rich, glowing ebony, and her long purple braid swings over her shoulder, a ribbon of color that seems to move with a life of its own. Her eyes shine bright and keen, reflecting the moonlight like polished amethyst.

I tilt my head, and my ears twitch as Lorna's fingers move, weaving the enchantment. Lark's form melts into something impossibly familiar: the sharp angles of Selvara's face, the pale skin, the dark hair, the cruel curve of her lips.

Even her voice takes on that imperious cadence, cool and commanding, drifting through the cold air to brush against my ears, and I feel the pack tense with me. "Do I look like her?" she whispers.

"You're ready," Lorna says with a nod.

Lark steps forward, each movement filled with deception, speaking like Selvara. Her voice is a smooth sound of command threaded with familiarity. "I'm here now, my lovelies. Come into the moonlight. It's time."

The twelve witches are inside the cavern, unaware that the Selvara before them is not their queen, but a shadow of Lark, an illusion wrought from deep, ancient magic.

I can see them smile, eager, expectant; the loyalty Selvara has cultivated in them is a living thing, and it bends now to our advantage. They follow quickly, the first stepping out into the snow, then the next, drawn by the spell and the illusion, until the entire coven gathers just outside the mouth of the cave, bathed in silver moonlight.

From the nearby ridge, we watch in silence. The witches step fully into the clearing now, their pale faces lifted to the moon. The air is thick with magic, with the tension of their obedience, and I know the moment of confrontation is nearly at hand. From our hidden ridge, with the snow frozen and glittering around us, the plan stands ready. Lorna and Lark hold their dangerous, perfect deception, and we wait as predators poised in the dark, the night sky closing in around the Montelune peaks.

The witches sing, their voices rising in a dark harmony, chanting an old song that twists through the mountains like smoke curling in the cold air. Moonlight spills across the clearing, glinting on their alabaster faces and the sharp points of their teeth.

Xamara brushes against me. White fur shimmers in the frost. *"Soon, this will all be over."*

Just then, one of my warriors loses his footing and slips into the corner of the moonlight. One of the witches catches sight of him, her eyes filling with horror. She shrieks, cutting through the night like shattered glass. "Nightborn! Now!"

From the shadowed mouth of the cave, darkness floods out, hundreds of Nightborn swarming us. Their eyes gleam red in the moonlight, which gleams off their fangs. Bodies take to flight with unnatural grace. The mountains quake beneath the sudden violence.

I leap. The snow explodes beneath me as I land. My claws cut deep into one of the beasts. Xamara is at my side, her white form a streak of light and frost, and together we roll into the first cluster of Nightborn. Jaws snap; teeth clash against their sinew. Mason and Simeon split to flank left, Jax and Zara surge to the right, and Kai drives forward through the heart of the swarm. The rogues weave through, Havelock smashing into the closest, Seamus and Mac cutting across, and Ivy slashing with precision.

The clash is a storm of movement: moonlight on silver teeth, black fur blending into shadows, sparks of magic from stray spells thrown by the coven. Every sense is alive, the air sharp with the scent of blood and snow, the screams and snarls twisting around the peaks. I protect Xamara at all costs. I growl, lunging through a throng, sinking my fangs into a Nightborn's throat and turning it to ash.

The witches, still in their moonlit circle, clutch each other, chanting frantically to summon aid, but our attack breaks the first wave. I hear Lorna and Lark's voices threading through the wind in a murmur of preparation. Lark moves along the ridge with the other witches while Lorna stays hidden from them. Both of their fingers are working over their satchels, drawing the threads of power.

As the tide of Nightborn ebbs slightly under our assault, Lark's form shifts, the illusion of Selvara dissolving. She emerges with her identity no longer hidden, wearing a lavender gown that catches the moonlight and a silk cloak that brushes the frosty ground. Beside her, Lorna emerges with her satchel in her hands, her dark eyes focused on her work. The snow falls around them, the cliff behind them framing their figures like a painting.

A whisper of confusion sounds through the witches as they try to discern where their leader may be. They have gathered near the mouth of the cave, not sure what to do, and disorganized without the queen.

The night air trembles with the clash of magic and fury as more Nightborn surge from the cave, their fangs reflecting the moonlight. My pack explodes into action, and Xamara lunges ahead, a streak of white in the dark, scattering a group of Nightborn.

I leap over a jagged boulder, finding my balance in the snow, and land in the midst of a group of Nightborn, ripping, snapping, my fangs sinking into their flesh. The witches screech behind them in a chorus of madness. Voices drip with venom, their spells hissing through the winter air.

The battle surges in a storm of black fur and red eyes, claws and teeth, magic and hate. The ground is torn with blood mixing in the snow.

Lorna and Lark move with purpose to a higher cliff. They weave shapes in the air, murmuring words as old as these very mountains, and while I can't see the magic take shape, I feel the pulse of it, the rhythm of power building, pressing down on the Nightborn, bending the air around them.

I bite into a Nightborn's shoulder and tear. Havelock throws one against the rocks. Seamus dives past another. Mason's claws cut through a dark creature's face. Ivy's speed is a blur, and Mac is a shadow hammering down the enemy. Every movement counts, every strike a promise: we will not falter. My warriors move with precision.

The witches shriek, summoning what remains of their power, but the mountain seems to hum beneath my paws, responding to the spell above, twisting the night itself.

A sudden brilliance cuts through the darkness. Golden sun explodes into the night, a shaft of light ripping the sky open. The night sky fractures, clouds scattering, and for a breath, the world is suspended in a blinding orb of yellow brilliance. Bathed in daylight that should never have been, illuminating horror and hope alike, the sky vibrates with heat and radiance, sharp and pure, and I feel a surge of power crash over the battlefield like a wave.

Nightborn and witches shriek as their bodies crumble into ash, curling upward on the wind, scattering into silver motes that shimmer in the suddenly conjured sunlight. I blink against the brightness, staggering back. The nightmare dissolves before my eyes. Magic heats my fur, but the wolf shifters are safe from the spell.

The field falls into a stillness broken only by the labored breaths of my mate, my packmates, and the rogues. Snow falls lightly to the scorched ground. I lift my head toward the higher cliff where Lorna and Lark stand with their hands still raised, the final glow of magic catching the light of a new dawn. They watch, calm and commanding, as the remnants of the war fade into ash. The Montelune peaks gleam in golden light, and at last, the battle, the war, and the terror of the coven are over.

25

HONOR

The forest thins, Blackwater Castle coming into view ahead of us as we run the last stretch through the snow, our pace quick. After a long night on the move, the sight of Julian's stronghold brings a spiritual lift to the group. The coven has been destroyed, the Nightborn have been defeated, and we are returning to his fortress victorious, with no remaining threat at our backs.

Now only Selvara remains.

I keep my place near the front, Julian at my side, his warriors fanned out behind us. The five rogues pad along with us. Havelock and Mac run ahead. Seamus, Ivy, and Lark patrol the tree line.

I think about Ian as we move through the snow, his absence an ache in my chest. He should be running beside us, teasing the rogues, laughing at something small to break the tension, and I realize how quiet the journey feels without him.

We push forward through the last stretch of forest, the castle walls growing taller with every stride. Julian's pace never slows, and I match him, feeling the energy of the pack behind us when the gates come into view, the first sounds of activity drifting from inside, signaling that the stronghold is awake and waiting for our return.

"Almost home," Julian says.

The words hang between us, part reassurance, part warning. Crossing into Blackwater lands means finally dealing with Selvara, my stepmother, whose schemes set everything in motion. We know she's weakened, but we can't underestimate what she has done or the consequences of her actions.

Julian's strength ebbs off him as we move toward the castle, a reminder that I'm not facing what's inside alone.

We crest the final rise. The gates stand open, with guards lined along the walls. When they spot their Alpha, they straighten, relief breaking across their faces.

"Ian should be walking through these gates with us," I say.

"We'll honor him," Julian responds.

The courtyard fills with the light of dawn as we cross it. The sky is washed in gray clouds and soft yellow streams. It's the kind of morning that would normally feel peaceful. Instead, everyone moves with the urgency of a pack trying to understand that we've brought home a victory, but there's still work for their Alpha to attend to.

Julian dismisses his warriors, and the rogues fall in behind me, then slip away toward their chambers to shift, wash, dress, eat, and breathe. They deserve the rest. All of us do.

Julian meets my eyes. *"I'll meet you at your chambers, and we'll deal with Selvara together."*

"Of course. Thank you, Julian," I say with a deep breath, and we move toward opposite stairwells.

I step into my chamber. A fire burns in the hearth, and a bath has been drawn. On the bed lies a gown of black and silver silk, the colors of Julian's pack. Julian must have sent word ahead to have everything ready, which is remarkably considerate, especially after a battle. He was still thinking of my comfort and my needs.

My bones ache from the fight as I shift. Fur recedes, bones snap into place, and moments later, I stand on bare feet. I sink into the bath, the water scented with lavender and peppermint, and wash my hair. As badly as I want to soak, I have work to do, so I pull myself out of the bath, dry off, and pin my hair up before slipping into a black-and-silver gown.

I want to check in with Willow to see if Ian is still hanging on. But I don't. I can't bear to. Until it's confirmed that we've lost him, I can continue to pretend that he's going to be all right.

When Julian meets me outside my door, he's already dressed, his hair still damp from a wash.

"Are you all right? Are you ready?" he asks.

"Yes," I say.

"You look beautiful," he says, then adds, "I'll be right here with you, every step." He offers his arm. I take it, letting him guide me forward.

We walk together to the lower levels. Torches burn in sconces on the walls. The air grows cooler and heavier the deeper we go. The dungeon is still, except for the four guards posted at the cell.

Selvara hangs from chains bolted into the wall, her legs barely supporting her. Her power has been drained almost completely, and what remains isn't enough to threaten, but serves as a reminder of what she once was. Her skin is gray, her breath shallow, as she lifts her head with effort, her eyes barely open.

Julian steps forward first, his voice filled with authority. "Selvara, you have two choices. You can leave this cell and live in a room under guard in the turret. You will use no magic. Not a spark." He nods toward the floor beneath her feet. "Or you can stay here until your life ends. But if you attempt to use your powers one more time, I will make the decision for you—and it will be none of the above."

I add, "Your coven is gone. Every last one of them. The Nightborn all turned to ash, too. There's nothing left to scheme for."

"No! No! That can't be!" she screams. Her voice cracks as she thrashes against the chains. "You—how could you take it all? Everything I built, everything I controlled!" Her hands strike at the air, fists curling and unclenching, but the chains hold her fast. "This isn't fair! None of it is fair!" Her words tumble out, ragged, full of fury and disbelief, each one a raw strike against the stepdaughter she thought she ruled.

"Yes," Julian says. "You gave us their location. We lured them out of their cave, and every last one of them burned in our conjured sunlight."

Tears stream down her face. She shouts, trembling in the chains, "We were banished, scattered, imprisoned in different cells across Vaeloria and Hexeton. The kingdoms thought cages would hold us. Then the vampire shifters came. They agreed to a trade: a bite for freedom. We became their familiars, bound but powerful. The Moonfang blood kept us alive." She turns to me. "That's why I married your father, child. Not love. Necessity."

The words hit me, and my knees buckle before I can brace myself. I sway, my vision blurring, and Julian's hands are suddenly on my arms, holding me upright. I lean against him, trembling, and for a moment I can't form a single thought.

Selvara lifts her head again. Darkness ignites behind her eyes. I see a fragile, desperate spark of black magic, and realize too late what she intends. Her fingers twitch. A thin thread of evil braids together. It's weak but aimed directly at my heart.

Julian moves before I do, fury snapping through him like a whip as he steps between us. "Enough! Take her outside! Now!"

The ghost of black magic dissipates quickly now that she cannot reach me. Hitting Julian with her magic will do her no good.

The guards surge forward, unlocking the chains and dragging her out into the corridor. Selvara shrieks.

"Julian—" I start.

He shakes his head, his jaw locked. "She's made her choice."

We follow the guards up the stairs and into the courtyard. Dawn has fully broken; sunlight spills over the stones in a bright, rising tide.

When they push her into the light, Selvara's body recoils, and a scream tears from her throat, manic and wild. Her skin bubbles and cracks as if fire runs beneath it, and then it begins to crumble, flaking away in gray-white shards. Ash lifts from her arms and hair, drifting like smoke caught in the wind, curling and twisting before vanishing into the sunlit air. Her screams fracture as her form disintegrates, leaving nothing behind but the echo of fury and ruin.

Her scream cuts off.

A gust of morning wind scatters the last of her across the courtyard stones, and Selvara is gone forever.

The courtyard is still settling, the ashes barely dispersed, when I hear a message through the mind-link–urgent and unmistakably Willow.

"Xamara! Please come to the healing center now!"

I look at Julian. "Willow needs me. It sounds important."

Julian doesn't ask why. "Let's go."

We cross the courtyard quickly. Doors blur past us, the early morning bustle of the castle fading under the pounding of our footsteps. We turn down the hallway that leads to the healers' wing, and before we reach the doorway, I can already hear Willow's sobs.

Inside, the steam-filled air smells of herbs. Helena and Willow stand beside the table next to Ian's silver wolf.

He's laid out carefully, his fur brushed back with his body wrapped in blankets as if they're trying to warm someone that can't be warmed. I saw him fall. I felt the truth of it in the empty space he left behind.

Willow's cries fill the room, and she covers her mouth. I cross the space in three strides and pull her into my arms. She clings to me, trembling.

I expect grief, but when I look past her, I see Ian's ribcage rise and then fall. Again, a rise and fall.

I stare, unable to speak.

He opens his eyes, looking around dazed.

"Willow," I whisper, "He's—he's breathing. He's alive!"

I release her from my embrace as Willow tries to speak but chokes on another sob. Helena rubs her arm and answers for both of them. "We worked on him for hours. We refused to give up. His heart would not beat. But then shortly after dawn—" She looks at me, tears brimming her eyes. "He suddenly began to breathe."

She looks from me to Julian, searching for answers she doesn't have.

Julian looks at me, his mind already moving. "Dawn," he says slowly. Then he looks at Ian. "It was when Selvara died."

I know it's true. The darkness that evaporated the moment Selvara's life ended left Ian's body, too.

"When she died, the spell was broken, and Ian's life was restored," I say.

Tears blur my vision as I lay a hand on his silver fur. He's warm. I bow my head against him, pressing close, overwhelmed by the fact that he is really here.

"Ian," I reach for him through the mind-link. *"Can you hear me?"*

A sluggish, familiar voice drifts back. *"Yes, Xamara. Please, don't cry. I'm all right, just tired. My body is sore as hell, but I'm alive."*

A laugh floats out of me, impossible to hold back. *"You saved my life,"* I tell him. *"And you're still here. I'm so damn happy you're here."*

His tail thumps once.

Julian exhales beside me, wrapping a comforting arm around me.

Ian is alive.

The news spreads through the castle faster than wildfire: Ian didn't die, and the coven is gone forever. By midmorning, the entire courtyard is buzzing, the news leaping from warrior to scout, from servant to shepherd, until it reaches every edge of Blackwater lands.

A celebration is called for. Massive tables are carried into the courtyard, then covered with bread, meat, fresh cheeses, and bright bowls of berries. Farmers bring barrels of elderberry cider and corn whiskey. Shepherds arrive with gifts of wool blankets and gratitude that their herds are now safe. Warriors raise cups in victory and joy. Music, laughter, and conversation swell throughout the castle grounds.

The seven rogues move through the crowd together, even Ian, who is glued to Willow's side, and their spirits are lighter than I've ever seen. They're greeted with cheers and plates piled high. Even the smallest children know their names now, tugging at their sleeves and asking what a Nightborn looks like up close. The rogues grin, proud but a little shy, not used to open praise.

Ian sits amongst friends, draped in blankets with a bowl of broth before him. Every few minutes, someone stops by–warriors offering him well wishes, healers checking on him, and villagers bowing their heads in thanks. He endures it all with a tired, crooked smile, his eyes drifting toward me often, as if he's reassuring himself that we both survived.

When Julian steps forward, the whole courtyard quiets. He lifts his voice, strong and proud. "Today, we honor every warrior who fought with us. Every guard who held the line at home. Every rogue who bled beside us." His gaze lands on Ian. "And we honor Ian, who gave his life, and gained it back, saving Xamara, by facing darkness head on with bravery and sacrifice."

A roar rises from the crowd, echoing off the castle walls. Ian lowers his head, overcome, and Julian lets the noise wash over him before raising a hand again.

"And this blessed day, we honor two more. Lorna and Lark." He gestures for them to come forward.

The gorgeous enchantresses emerge, both blushing and beaming. When they step into the sun, the courtyard erupts a second time with cheering, clapping, and people shouting their names like they're legends already carved in stone.

Julian nods to them. "Their brilliance ended the war. Their courage brought dawn to Montelune when we needed it most. That light destroyed the coven and the Nightborn. They brought peace to many kingdoms."

Lorna wipes at her eyes. Lark beams like she's still holding the sun itself. Children swarm them with questions about the bottles of light, the magic, and the way the sky burst into a corona of light.

By sunset, the musicians are still playing lively tunes, bonfires burn in great rings, and every shadow in the courtyard feels safer than it has in weeks. Julian and I take our places at the pair of thrones set at the far end of the courtyard. The castle behind us glows orange in the firelight, the people dancing below a living vision of happiness and tranquility.

I lean back, watching the rogues, the pack, and the kingdom that survived. Julian takes my hand, and the thought rises: What will we do now?

What will become of all of us now that the war is over? What does

Blackwater's future hold? And what becomes of Moonfang now that its Luna has burned with the coven?

I squeeze Julian's hand, letting the victory and Ian's return fill my heart, and the images of the battle and Selvara's schemes fade away. Nothing exists beyond this night and my mate's hand in mine, the life we've reclaimed, and the path that stretches before us.

2 6

MOTHERS AND LUNAS

The victory celebration in the courtyard fades away as Julian and I step inside the castle. Music drifts faintly through the halls, but tonight, the inside of the castle feels like it belongs only to us.

He opens the door to his chambers with a lustful look that tells me he knows exactly what I need, and I step inside, letting him guide me forward. The fire in the hearth has dimmed, embers glowing like molten gold. He locks the door, and by the time we reach the bed, our clothes are on the floor.

Julian lays me on my back on the bed and kisses me. I reach for his cock, stroking it as he trails kisses along my jawline over to my earlobe. His muscles look mouthwateringly delicious, and I can't help leaning up to bite his bicep. Mischief dances in his eyes as he parts my legs, lowering his lips to my folds.

He looks up at me with his beautiful brown eyes and sucks my clit into his mouth. I moan, caught in the waves of sensation he's provoking, and move instinctively with him as he flicks his tongue over my sweet spot. He reaches up to tease my breasts, and I cry out in pure pleasure.

He moves his hands to the backs of my legs and lifts, giving himself a different angle. Julian sucks and licks my most sensitive parts, and I moan louder, pressing the back of his head so that he's closer to me as my body teeters on the edge of ecstasy.

Then, he pushes two of his fingers inside me, and I arch my back, my body releasing in a rush of liquid heat that leaves me breathless.

After I climax, he softly runs his fingers up and down my slit. "You're so beautiful when you come," he murmurs, his voice low and full of desire.

When I finally catch my breath, I push him onto his back and straddle him. I lower myself onto his cock and lean forward, moving slowly at first, savoring every inch of our closeness. He takes one of my breasts in his mouth, fully aware of how every teasing motion drives me wild. He starts gently, then increases the pressure, guiding me with the sensations he creates, and I respond, moving faster and harder with him. He feels so good inside me, every movement making my body burn with need. I can feel another climax rising.

"Julian, please don't stop," I gasp. He hungrily takes one nipple in his mouth while pinching the other and thrusting into me exactly how I need it.

I lean forward even further, letting him take over, his body beneath me, pounding harder and deeper, every thrust hitting me perfectly, making my vision blur with pleasure.

A moment later, I feel my fangs extending. I bury my head in Julian's neck and bite down. At the same time, I feel his teeth in my flesh. It doesn't hurt, though. From now on, his mark will claim me as his, and the world will know he belongs to me.

Sitting up, I moan, my body quaking on top of him as he drives into me from beneath, every thrust pushing us over the edge together, and he groans, losing himself inside me, warmth spreading through me with his final grunt of release.

We both settle onto the bed side by side, still flushed and spent. He wraps an arm around me, pulling me close, and I feel the warmth of his chest beneath my cheek. "I love you, Luna of Blackwater," he whispers.

"I love you, too," I say, my heart soaring at the sound of Julian calling me Luna of Blackwater.

I fall asleep in his arms, feeling seen and cherished like never before.

I WAKE IN JULIAN'S BED. HE'S ALREADY AWAKE, WATCHING ME WITH A lazy smile. He gently brushes a thumb across my cheek, and murmurs, "Good morning, my beautiful Luna. I'm going to send orders through the mind-link. Servants will have a bath ready for you in your chambers, a fresh gown laid out, and the kitchens will start breakfast for us and the rogues."

I nuzzle closer, grateful for his constant attention and love. "Thank you," I whisper.

He smiles and kisses me before climbing out of bed. I can't help but take in every inch of him. His chiseled ass and strong back muscles make me wish we could stay in bed all day. Unfortunately, today we have work to do.

I rise slowly, still feeling the echo of sleep and last night's fire. When I make it to my chamber, the bath is drawn, and steam rises in the air. I wash and dress in a simple blue gown.

Julian meets me at my door and escorts me to breakfast. When we enter the dining hall, the seven rogues are already sitting at the table, and the smell of ham, eggs, and toast and jam fills the air.

Julian pulls out my chair, I sit down at the table, and when the room is settled enough to hear him clearly, Julian makes an announcement. "Havelock, if you're willing, I'd like you to serve as my head general."

The rogues' brows lift, then he nods once. "My loyalty is to you, Alpha."

Julian turns to Lark. "Would you consider joining Lorna as a sorceress? She could use someone with your knowledge of magic."

Lark grins. "Absolutely. I'd love that."

"Willow," Julian continues, "Helena says you are a gifted healer. If you want to work with her, the position is yours."

She nods enthusiastically. "Of course. I'd like that very much. Thank you, Alpha."

"Seamus and Mac," Julian says, looking between the two, "would you take charge of a new set of patrols? Your tracking skills are unmatched."

Mac smirks. "We can handle that."

Seamus nods. "Count us in."

Then Julian's gaze lands on Ivy. "If you're willing, I'd like you to train the young women to fight."

Ivy sets her teacup on the table, a smile blooming on her face. "I'll do it."

Finally, he turns to Ian. "I'd like you to serve as Xamara's bodyguard."

Ian glances at me, then back at Julian. "I'd be honored, Alpha."

One by one, I look at them, seeing a mixture of pride, excitement, and respect in their faces. My chest tightens with warmth as my heart melts, seeing them claim their new places, knowing Julian trusts them.

Julian sits at the head of the table, and as we eat breakfast, the conversation moves to Moonfang Pack. "We definitely need to go check on them," Julian says. "The spell that bound their warriors must be broken now that the black magic is gone."

"I only hope they greet us with open arms rather than fangs like last time we were there," I add.

He reaches across the table and takes my hand. "I'm sure they will be back to normal, but just in case, I'll have Mason round up the warriors here. After breakfast, we leave for Moonfang. All of us together."

Breakfast continues, laughter and conversation flowing between bites and sips of warm tea, but my gaze keeps drifting to Julian. Every decision he makes, every plan he lays, is laced with care and consideration. He is thoughtful and kind in ways that soothe me, even as my mind spins with the uncertainty of the future, the journey to Moon-fang, and the battles we have yet to face.

THE FOREST BLURS AROUND US AS WE RUN, WOLVES SLIPPING THROUGH the snow, satchels strapped to our backs. Julian leads, his black coat cutting through the winter woods, the rogues weaving around us in perfect sync, their shapes familiar and loyal.

The Gleabhain River comes into view, rushing dark, churning and curving through the trees. Its current is faster than usual, swollen from the night's thaw, and the roar reaches even over the sound of our paws. Julian's voice threads through the mind-link, carrying an order to his warriors. *"Stay close together as we cross. Watch your footing, and keep the pack tight."*

The rogues freeze mid-stride, their ears pricked, and their eyes darting between one another. *"Did you just... hear that?"* Lark's voice is filled with disbelief.

"Alpha, we hear you," Havelock calls.

"Thank the Moon Goddess! It'll be so much easier to be able to hear everyone," Ivy says, her tail flicking.

As the other rogues chime in, I can feel their astonishment ripple through the mind-link, their thoughts bright and sharp as they test it, calling back to Julian, who must realize for the first time that the rogues have joined the connection. We are all linked now that the rogues have been accepted into Blackwater Pack.

As we enter Moonfang territory, the castle waits in the distance, and I know the people within have been living under Selvara's rule for too long. I slow my pace as we crest the rise, and Julian looks at me.

"You wait here," I tell him. *"I'll go to the castle alone. We don't want to bring the whole army and alarm the people unnecessarily."*

"I trust your instincts, Xamara, but keep me updated and let me know the second you sense trouble."

I nod a promise and then slip through the trees, my satchel falling from my back with a soft thump. I quickly shift and dress.

I walk toward the castle, my nerves prickling. My heart beats faster. I'm unsure how the pack will react to seeing me. Will they accept me? Will they resist? Will Selvara's spell linger despite the victory we claimed?

People look up as I draw near. There are servants carrying firewood, stable hands tending to the horses, and children playing near the gates. Recognition sparks in their eyes, and smiles spread quickly. "Princess Xamara!" someone calls. Others wave and call greetings, their voices warm and bright, and I can't help but return the smiles, my heart lifting at the familiar faces I haven't seen in so long.

I push through the main doors, the castle quiet around me. Servants and warriors glance up, then pause, their eyes filling with awe as they recognize me. "Princess!" one calls, and a few others bow their heads, stepping aside to let me pass.

A guard approaches, and I ask him to summon Beta Branok. He nods once and moves quickly down the hall. A few minutes later, he returns with the head warrior at his side.

The Beta's eyes wander over me, one narrowed slightly in scrutiny. His mouth is pursed as he ponders what I will ask of him. No doubt, he realizes he has done a disservice to my family. But I am far too aware that he had no decision in the matter.

"Please, Beta Branok, I need to speak with you," I say. "Selvara wasn't a shifter. She was a vampiric witch, using black magic to control the pack. She's dead, and the spell is broken."

He crosses his arms and lets out a deep breath. "Well, that certainly changes things," he says. "We were wondering where she'd disappeared to. If her reign is over... I suppose that makes you the Luna, Xamara."

I nod, knowing the first step in reclaiming Moonfang has begun. I reach out to Julian through the mind-link. *It's done. Selvara's spell is broken, and I am Luna of Moonfang.*

Julian responds immediately. *Xamara, that's incredible. We'll shift, dress, and meet you at the castle.*

"The Alpha of Blackwater Pack and his warriors are approaching," I warn the Beta. "But they hold no ill will regarding the fight that took place yesterday. We understand that Moonfang was under a spell. Come, let's greet them."

I wait just outside the castle, Beta Branok at my side. He moves down the line of guards, nodding firmly as he announces that I am their Luna and that Alpha Julian and the Blackwater pack are to be allowed inside.

The gates swing open, and Julian steps into the courtyard in his human form, wearing a regal outfit, with his warriors close behind him. He stops before me and inclines his head in a playful, exaggerated bow. "Your Majesty," he says with a grin, his eyes alight, "Luna of Moonfang suits you well, but Luna of Blackwater suits you better."

He kisses my temple, and butterflies leap in my stomach at the thought of the two of us ruling our kingdoms together.

As the Moonfang people recognize the rogues, their faces light up with disbelief and joy. Friends and family rush forward with their arms open wide, calling their names, and years of separation vanish in an instant. Tight hugs are shared, and laughter bursts freely as the rogues are welcomed home at last, their exile erased by the return to their places among those who never stopped waiting for them.

Selvara is gone, the spell broken, and the people have a new Luna. I move through the crowd with Julian at my side, greeting warriors and friends I haven't seen in weeks. Every servant offers a kind word, every soldier a respectful bow or nod.

One of the older war generals steps forward, his robes brushing the ice-crusted stones, his demeanor respectful. "Luna Xamara," he begins, "now that Selvara is dead, you must see the eldest of our pack. Elder Orlena, who helped bring you into this world, will help guide you. Her home is on the north side of the merchant's square. Please, go visit her at once."

I nod and thank him. Julian falls into step beside me as we leave the courtyard. Together, we walk toward the north side of the merchant square. The street is quiet this morning, and at the far end, a small house stands on the corner next to the bakery. I've passed it countless times over the years but have never been inside.

I knock, and an old woman appears, her back bent with years, but she has bright, friendly eyes.

"Princess Xamara? Is that you?" she asks, surprise and caution threaded through each word.

"Yes, it's me," I say firmly. "Well, I am Luna now. Are you Elder Orlena?"

"I am," she says. "How did you come to be the Luna?"

"Selvara was never one of us, and she is gone."

Her face relaxes, relief washing through her features. She steps aside, beckoning us in. "Come. Sit. There is much you must know."

I follow her inside, Julian close behind, and the warm cottage is instantly comforting. We sit near the fire, and Elder Orlena offers us each a mug of tea.

"Your mother's name was Desdemona," she begins. "I was her midwife, and I was there when you were born. The day you came into this world, the snow fell in large, sparkling flakes just like diamonds themselves. Luna Desdemona named you Xamara because it means *diamonds*."

My heart beats out of my chest and tears threaten as I remember the dream I had.

"She was taken from you," the elder continues, "because Selvara put a curse on all the Lunas in the area that year. Her intent was to weaken and eventually kill them. Your mother, Desdemona, was one of the first lost."

I reach for Julian's hand, finding it immediately.

"I'm so sorry," the elder says, her voice trembling. "I was terrified of the coven. I couldn't tell you sooner. I prayed to the Moon Goddess for this day, that Selvara would finally be gone, and that the throne would return to you as rightful heir."

"Thank you," I say quietly. "Thank you for telling me."

Her lips tremble, and she nods. "Your path was always meant to return here, Luna Xamara. Now, the pack has you, and the curses that haunted us are gone."

Julian's eyes drop, a shadow of sadness crossing his features. "My mother must've been one of the Lunas the coven killed, too." His eyes glisten, and I feel the loss carried across years and bloodlines through our bond.

He slides his arm around my shoulders, and the three of us sit together, letting the truth of the past prepare us for the future. In this moment, I feel the pulse of Moonfang and Blackwater beating in my heart, the echo of the mothers and Lunas who came before me, and the determination to honor them.

2 7

TWO BECOME ONE

The village streets are filled with merchants and pack members. As we walk back to the courtyard in the center of Moonfang Pack territory, I hold Xamara's hand, trying to keep my composure.

"I still can't believe it," I mutter. "All this time, we didn't know what illness overtook my mother. She died because of a curse. A dark and evil curse."

My mate looks up at me, her eyes shadowed with grief. "I'm sorry, Julian," she whispers. "It's terrible."

The memory of my mother's death is still razor sharp. When I was younger, I always imagined her living to an old age, surrounded by family, but then she was taken when I was so young… by a curse no one knew how to fight.

"It's difficult," I say. "But we will carry this together, and we owe it to our people to remain strong."

She nods. "We should talk about the future of our packs."

"You're right. You can't be Luna of two different packs easily."

"I know." She looks at me with a new spark in her eyes. "I've been thinking the same thing. What if we merged the packs? Just think of how much stronger we would be together."

I nod, feeling a rush of relief. "We'll run it by Mason and Moonfang's Beta first and get their input, but I think it's the right choice. Our people deserve unity, not division."

When we return to the Moonfang courtyard, we greet Mason first and tell him our plan.

"The two of you are born leaders," he says. "I think this could work out well for both packs."

Xamara leads me across the courtyard to where a man is speaking with Havelock. "Julian, this is Beta Branok," she says. "Beta, this is Alpha Julian of Blackwater Pack. He's my fated mate, and I will soon be his Luna."

I step forward. "Beta Branok," I say, nodding.

Branok shakes my hand.

"Beta, we need your counsel," Xamara says. "I can't be Luna of both packs. Alpha Julian and I believe it would be best if we combined our forces. Do you think the two should merge?"

Branok considers the idea for a moment before speaking. "This is a decision for you, my Luna. Although I will say, nothing can be as bad as being ruled by the evil and selfish Selvara, and I do believe the packs will be stronger together."

The decision is made. Relief passes between us in a glance, unspoken but complete. Together, we step onto the platform in the courtyard, and Xamara lifts her voice, clear and proud, declaring the future of our leadership.

"Warriors of Blackwater! Warriors of Moonfang, hear this! From this day forward, Moonfang and Blackwater Packs will become one!"

A celebratory roar erupts, reverberating off the stone walls, filling my chest with a comfort that almost makes me forget the ache of loss.

I kiss Xamara's hand, smiling at her. Together, we've faced grief and fear, and together, we've forged a new future. Our packs, our people, our families, will all grow as one.

A few days have passed since the merger, and Abrenna Castle feels alive in a way I never imagined it could. Blackwater and Moonfang are no longer two separate packs or two separate kingdoms. We are one, united under Xamara and me. We have decided to call the new pack Blackfang Pack.

The first days were tense, full of careful discussions and delicate negotiations. Every decision needed to account for the warriors, healers, merchants, farmers, shepherds, and everyone else in the two kingdoms. But with Xamara at my side, calm and decisive as ever, and the support of the new leaders, it has gone smoother than I dared hope.

Spring has arrived. The snow has melted, and the air carries the scent of wet earth and new growth. Xamara moves among the leaders with authority, her presence commanding respect. She belongs here as the Luna by my side, and together, we are building something stronger than either pack has ever known.

These past days have been exhausting, but in a good way. It's the kind of exhaustion that comes from building something lasting–something that matters. We've worked through the logistics, assigned responsibilities, smoothed over disagreements, and watched the leaders of both former packs grow comfortable with one another. I've seen warriors of Moonfang share laughter with Blackwater hunters, shepherds trading advice across fields. Unity is taking hold, and I can feel it in the pulse of the villages and in the rhythm of the people's lives.

Tonight will be the crowning moment of it all. Under the full moon in the Gleabhain Valley, we will celebrate the joining of the packs with the worship of the Moon Goddess. The valley will be lit with lanterns and banners with the new pack name fluttering in the spring breeze. Music will drift across the grass, mingling with the scent of food, the sound of laughter and cheer rising above the glimmer of torchlight. It will be a night of ceremony, joy, and unity.

I glance at Xamara as she moves past me, her blue eyes bright, her dark hair blowing in the breeze as she walks through the garden. She doesn't notice me watching, and I let myself take in every detail of her beauty, every curve of her body, and every little way she moves. Tonight, I will kneel before her, in front of our people and under the blessing of the Moon Goddess. I've been planning it, rehearsing the words in my mind and imagining the feel of her hand in mine when I ask her to be my wife.

But for now, there's time to savor this quiet before the storm of celebration. The pack has never been stronger, and I can feel the excitement in the air, the anticipation buzzing through the warriors and villagers alike. The scent of spring blossoms drift down from the hills while bonfires are being lit, fiddles tuned, and songs rehearsed. Tonight will mark the birth of a new era for Moonfang and Blackwater, and I will finally have the chance to tell Xamara what has been in my heart since the moment I saw her, a snow-white wolf fighting for her life. The valley waits for us. The full moon rises, silver and brilliant over the river. Tonight, everything changes.

THE GLEABHAIN VALLEY IS ALIVE WITH LIGHT AND SOUND. LANTERNS swing gently in the spring breeze, casting golden pools over the grass. Bonfires crackle, their flames licking the night sky. Music drifts across the valley, fiddles and fifes mingling with the laughter of warriors, villagers, and rogues alike. Everywhere I look, I see joy and celebration, but my eyes are only on Xamara, radiant in the glow of the full moon. She's never looked more alive, more beautiful, and my chest aches with the need to make her mine forever.

I take her hand as we reach the center of the gathering. "Xamara," I murmur, kneeling on one knee before her, "I have loved you since the very second I saw you. From this moment forward, I want nothing more than to walk through life with you by my side. Will you marry me?"

She gasps, tears brimming her eyes. "Yes," she whispers, and I feel her love wash over me in a perfect wave.

I slide the opal moonstone ring onto her finger, the gem reflecting the moonlight and sparkling like the first star of evening. She looks at it, then up at me, and I can't resist pulling her into a fierce, heart-stopping kiss. Around us, the valley erupts in cheers.

The music swells, and I take her hand. "Dance with me," I murmur. We move together under the full moon, our bodies swaying, hearts beating as one. She laughs, and her eyes are filled with contentment. I can't remember a moment when she's looked more beautiful, more like the Luna of my heart and our new pack.

Ian stays close, vigilant as ever, his eyes scanning the tree line, but he never interrupts, letting her smile and laugh without fear.

The night stretches on. Songs are sung, stories are shared, and the moon climbs higher. Finally, I lean close to Ian, lowering my voice. "Would you mind giving us a little privacy?" I ask.

He nods once, firm and loyal as ever. "Of course, Alpha."

I take Xamara's hand and lead her toward the edge of the valley, into the woods, the sound of the river flowing beside us. The moon glints off the black water.

I strip down without a word, shifting into my wolf form with a shiver of exhilaration. She laughs, a beautifully bold sound, before shedding her clothing and her human form as well. We race along the riverbank, the earth beneath our paws, the moon lighting our path.

She darts ahead, daring me to catch her, and I leap, powerful and fast, my tail whipping behind me. The night is ours, with the moon above us, the river beside us, and all that exists tonight is the joy, freedom, and thrill of marrying my fated mate.

28

LUNA XAMARA ABRENNA

I stand in the center of my bedchamber, trying to catch my breath, wearing my white silk wedding gown that glows like mist on the river. I am Luna of Moonfang, bride of Blackwater, joiner of two packs to make Blackfang, and in a few moments, I will walk toward the future I once thought I'd never have.

Behind me, the room rustles with movement and laughter. Willow twirls in her long green gown, her red hair blazing like autumn leaves set against spring. She pins a curl behind her ear and grins at her reflection, all bright energy and enthusiastic charm.

"You look stunning," Ivy tells Willow. "Like you're also about to ascend to a throne." Her blonde curls shimmer as she moves, her caramel skin radiant against her pale pink dress.

Lark adjusts the lavender cloak over her shoulders. Her ebony skin contrasts beautifully with the soft color, and her violet braid is woven with tiny amethysts that shimmer in the light. "She's the one ascending to a throne," Lark says, nodding toward me with a teasing smile. "We're just here to make sure she doesn't faint."

"I'm not going to faint," I say, though my heart is racing. The room is warm, buzzing, and alive. It feels like I'm standing in the center of a storm made of silk, jewels, perfume, and joy.

Helena steps toward me, carrying a small black box with silver trim. Her sapphire-blue gown falls in soft folds, and her dark curls are a crown atop her head with white lilies intertwined. "Hold still," she murmurs as she fastens a delicate bracelet around my wrist, the metal cool against my skin. "This was Julian's mother's. She gave it to me, and I want you to have it."

Tears fill my eyes. "Thank you so much, Helena." It's beautiful, a silver chain with a small wolf howling into the air.

Lorna's silver hair is braided down her back, and the orange gown she wears glows like firelight. "Your crown," she says, picking it up from the vanity. When she sets it on my head, her hands linger in my curls. "There. You're beautiful, Luna Xamara Abrenna."

I face the mirror, and for a moment, I barely recognize the woman looking back at me. My long, dark curls spill down my back. My moonstone-encrusted crown sits elegantly atop my head, not heavily the way I always imagined it would. My ivory gown skims the floor like flowing moonlight, and I look brand new. Not perfect or fearless, but ready for anything.

Willow clasps her hands together. "Xamara, you look—"

"Loved," Lark interrupts gently.

And something inside me changes. The nerves, the pressure, the old wounds are still there, but they aren't the loudest noise anymore.

I am loved, and I have been chosen. I am stepping into a life I get to build, not one forced upon me.

There's a light knock at the door, and a servant's voice calls through the wood. "Are you all ready in there?"

I meet my friends' eyes in the mirror. They smile back. "Yes," I say, lifting my chin. "We're ready."

The courtyard has been transformed. Sunlight spills across bright banners and fresh spring blossoms. Rows of chairs curve around the altar, where the red and gold of Moonfang and the black and silver of Blackwater are woven together in long sweeping ribbons and banners proclaim we are now Blackfang.

Today is a special day for all our nearby kingdoms. With the coven finally defeated, peace has returned to every realm, and now we celebrate our love before all the pack leaders, united as one. Alpha Kael and Maxiana of the Emerald Coast are seated near the front in bright sea-green cloaks. Alpha Leo and Roxy of Moonriver sit beside them with happy expressions on their faces. On the opposite side, Luna Xelina and Alpha Lazlo of Virechant, who traveled all the way across the Montelune Mountains to be here, offer me encouraging smiles. Next to them, Alpha King Canon and Luna Bexley look elegant and regal. The presence of these Alphas and Lunas makes the ceremony feel bigger than a wedding; it feels like history in the making.

I gasp when I step to the edge of the path. Julian looks incredibly handsome. He stands at the altar beside his Beta, Mason. Both wear fitted black suits trimmed with silver, the fabric catching every glint of light. Beta Branok waits between them, ready to officiate, his eyes filled with pride.

The ceremony begins as Havelock steps forward with Lark on his arm. He wears formal black while she moves like a lavender plume beside him. Her purple braid swings with each graceful step. Guests smile, and the music lifts even higher.

Next, Seamus walks with Willow. Her green gown ripples softly, almost glowing against her fiery red hair. Seamus looks both proud and terrified, which makes Willow beam even brighter.

Mac escorts Ivy after them. Ivy's pink gown glimmers like rose quartz, and her blonde curls bounce as she walks.

Jax offers Helena his arm. Helena's blue gown makes her eyes shine. Her crown of lilies shines white in the sunlight.

Simeon walks with Lorna next. Lorna's orange gown is like a molten sunset, and she carries herself with the confidence of someone who has seen the world change and survived it. Simeon looks determined to honor every step she takes.

Then the song changes, and guests rise. Ian offers me his arm, his black suit matching the others, crisp and clean. His expression holds pride and affection. "Ready?" he asks.

I nod, even though I can barely breathe, and we take the first step. A long silk train follows behind me.

Julian's eyes are wide, and I see him gasp as he takes me in. His gaze does not waver, and I feel the depth of every ounce of his love focused entirely on me.

When Ian places my hand in Julian's, acceptance blooms in my chest. Ian steps back. Julian strokes my hand with his thumb in a subtle gesture meant only for me.

Beta Branok begins the ceremony. His voice carries across the courtyard, clear and strong. He speaks of unity, loyalty, and the future we are choosing together. His words are formal, but they ring true in every part of me.

Julian lifts my hands gently. "I promise to guard your life as fiercely as I guard my pack," he says. "I promise to honor your strength and trust your wisdom. I promise to build a home where you are safe, loved, and free. I choose you, Xamara. Today, tomorrow, and every day after."

"I promise to stand beside you," I say. "I promise to protect our people and our future. I promise to speak truth, to love without fear, and to meet every challenge with you. I choose you, Julian. Forever."

Branok smiles. "You are now bound as mates and as Alpha and Luna. You may seal your union with a kiss."

Julian steps closer, and when he kisses me, the courtyard erupts with cheers. Joy crashes in around us while his lips move against mine with a promise that feels like forever. I am his, and he is mine.

The celebration begins the moment Julian and I step back down the aisle. Music swells, bright and joyful. Guests cheer and surround us as we are guided into the great hall where the feast has been prepared. The room glows with warm candlelight and rich spring colors. Tables overflow with meat, vegetables, fresh breads, early strawberries, honeyed pastries, and pitchers of sparkling cider. Laughter rises above the clatter of plates.

Julian keeps my hand in his as we weave between well-wishers. Every face beams with happiness. This day belongs to all of us, not just to the two of us who exchanged vows. Today marks the beginning of a unified future.

We sit at the head table with our closest friends, and for a moment, I simply let myself take it all in. Lark leans in to listen to Havelock with a wide smile. Ivy chatters excitedly with Mac, her curls bouncing each time she laughs. Helena lifts her glass with Lorna at her side. Mason listens to Simeon with patient amusement.

Willow stands near Seamus, who watches her with an affection he is not trying to hide in the least. I nudge Julian, and he follows my gaze. His smile deepens.

When the meal ends, and the musicians strike up a lively tune, the dancing begins. Julian pulls me into the center of the floor, and the pack forms a circle around us. His hands settle at my waist firmly, and my gown sways as he twirls me. I throw my head back and laugh because I can't hold the joy inside of me any longer. The world feels safe again. Nothing heavy presses on us anymore. Here, there is only hope, only love.

After several dances, the music softens, and I know it is time to toss the bouquet. I take a moment to gather the bridal flowers, a full arrangement of white lilies and light pink blooms, wrapped in foxglove and accented with baby's breath. All the single women of both packs gather behind me as I lift the bouquet over my head.

"One," I call.

The room quiets in anticipation.

"Two. Three!"

I toss it high, glancing over my shoulder as it arcs through the air in a perfect curve. Many hands reach for it, but the bouquet drops directly into Willow's outstretched hands. She gasps, pulling it against her chest, looking directly at Seamus. Laughter and cheers explode around her as she clutches it.

Julian leans close to my ear. "I saw that coming."

I smile because I did, too.

The dancing continues well into the evening. The sky outside deepens into a soft violet. As the musicians begin the final song, Julian and I slip out to the edge of the courtyard, preparing to leave for our honeymoon.

Before we step away, I notice movement near the gardens. Willow stands there with Seamus, the bouquet still in her hand. Seamus lowers himself to one knee. Willow lifts her free hand to her mouth, trembling. Even from this distance, I see the fire in her eyes as she nods yes.

Julian wraps his arm around my waist and pulls me gently against him. I rest my head against his shoulder.

"Love blooms in many ways tonight," he murmurs.

I lift my face and kiss him.

THE SILVERFEN CAVERN OPENS BEFORE US LIKE THE BREATH OF SOME ancient, sleeping goddess, warm, glowing, and alive. Mist curls around our ankles as Julian guides me inside, our fingers intertwined, our steps echoing against smooth stone. The air buzzes with magic.

Glowing crystals hang from the cavern walls in clusters, casting blue and violet light across the pools. The reflections ripple over Julian's face, painting him in glittering halos of pale fire. He looks otherworldly like this: half god, half myth, yet completely mine.

"Xamara," he gasps. "Look."

I follow his gaze. The largest pool lies before us, luminous and still, as if lit from its depths by the Moon Goddess Herself. Steam rises in silvery ribbons. The surface mirrors the cavern ceiling, creating the illusion that we are standing at the seam between two skies.

"It's pure magic," I breathe. "Stunning."

Julian squeezes my hand gently. "Not compared to you."

Normally, I'd tease him for saying something so cheesy, but tonight the words land differently.

We strip down and step into the water together. Heat envelops us instantly, sliding around our shoulders and spines, melting every ounce of lingering tension. Julian exhales, closing his eyes, the glow of the crystals brushing silver along his lashes.

I move closer until my body is flush against his beneath the surface. "We finally made it," I whisper.

He opens his eyes. "We did, and there's no one else I would rather be here with than you, Luna Xamara."

The water glows around us as if it is aware of the moment, brightening, deepening, illuminating the cavern in a soft pulse. Julian moves behind me and pulls me backward against him. My head fits beneath his chin, and he wraps his arms around my waist.

"Xamara, I've never been happier than I am at this moment," he says, and I hear the truth in his tone. "Never."

My throat tightens as I tilt my head back to look into his eyes. The light changes again, spilling lavender-blue across his face. He looks like a dream bathed in moon fire.

"I love you," I whisper.

"And I love you, my beautiful wife." Julian presses close behind me, his body warm against mine. His lips trace the curve of my neck, teasing, then claiming it, and I shiver. One hand cups my breast, kneading gently, pinching and rolling my nipple between his fingers. I tilt my head back into him, every touch sparking fire across my skin. His mouth moves along my throat, hot and demanding, and I feel him everywhere, pressing into me, impossibly close.

Instinctively, I lift my hips, grinding my backside against him. Julian moans as his hard cock presses against me, sliding against the curve of my ass. His hands don't leave my breasts, teasing them as he moves with me, his mouth still tracing the sensitive skin along my neck. The water ripples around us with each push and pull, and I'm more aroused with every touch.

I lift my arm, pressing it behind his head, pushing his mouth deeper into my neck. Julian groans and lifts me effortlessly, spinning me around so my legs wrap around his waist. He holds me there, his strong hands gripping my ass, and I clutch my breasts, offering them to him. His mouth finds them hungrily, sucking and teasing while his hardness slides up and down against my slit. Heat coils tight inside me. Every movement, every touch, sends shivers that pool low, and I lose myself in the rhythm and in the desire of us making love in the glowing, enchanted water.

I tilt my head back, giving him more, inviting him to take whatever he wants. He teases one nipple in slow circles with his tongue, and it takes my breath away. Then he closes his lips around it and sucks gently, then harder. I gasp and arch into him, my fingers digging into his shoulders.

He switches to the other breast, giving it the same worship, and the ache between my legs becomes a throb I can't ignore. I slide my hands down his chest, over the firm ridges of muscle, until I find him under the water and slide his cock inside of me.

"Xamara," he groans.

He grabs my hips and begins to move with powerful strokes that send waves sloshing around us. I meet every thrust, tangling my fingers in his hair, our mouths colliding in frantic kisses.

Julian thrusts into me, hard and deep, and I tighten around him, an orgasm ripping through me as I come on his cock. Every nerve is on fire as he holds me against him, driving me higher, his mouth still on my neck and breasts, gripping my hips tight.

He groans against my throat, thrusting harder and faster, and I feel him stiffen, his hips jerk, and he spills inside me. The friction drives me over the edge again, a second orgasm ripping through me as my walls clamp down around him.

Our breathing turns ragged as we wrap our arms around each other tight. My skin still tingles from every touch. For a moment, we stay still, letting the heat between us linger.

Eventually, we part, and he helps me out of the hot spring. I lean into him for balance as we step onto the smooth stones. We wrap ourselves up in waiting towels and walk arm in arm to our honeymoon quarters.

The chamber inside the cavern is comfortable and welcoming, with soft rugs underfoot, finely appointed furniture, and a fire burning in a carved stone hearth. Heavy wooden beams stretch across the ceiling for reinforcement, and a large four-poster bed dominates the center of the room, draped with rich linens.

Hand in hand, we move to the cave opening that overlooks the valley, the river rushing below. Julian's fingers brush across mine, and I am fully content. I think of everything we've survived: battles, witch covens, losses, victories, and the merging of packs.

When we settle back inside, curling up on the bed, Julian pulls me against him, and I rest my head on his shoulder. Here we are–alive, together, on our honeymoon, and ready to face everything the future holds. Tonight, I close my eyes knowing this is only the beginning.

And to think... it all started with a kiss that woke a sleeping princess.

ALSO BY BELLA MOONDRAGON

The Alpha King's Breeder series:

Bought by the Alpha: The Alpha King's Breeder Book 1 (free!)

Loved by the Alpha: The Alpha King's Breeder Book 2

Lost by the Alpha: The Alpha King's Breeder Book 3

Luna of the Alpha: The Alpha King's Breeder Book 4

Legacy of the Alpha: The Alpha Kings's Breeder Book 5

Daughter of the Alpha: The Alpha King's Breeder Book 6

Descendants of the Alpha: The Alpha King's Breeder Book 7

Shadow of the Alpha: The Alpha King's Breeder Book 8

Son of the Alpha: The Alpha King's Breeder Book 9

Spare of the Alpha: The Alpha King's Breeder Book 10

Claimed by the Alpha: The Alpha King's Breeder Book 11

Atonement for the Alpha King: The Alpha King's Breeder Book 12

Rejected by the Alpha: The Alpha King's Breeder Book 13

Abducted by the Alpha: The Alpha King's Breeder Book 14

Abandoned by the Alpha: The Alpha King's Breeder Book 15

Champion of the Alpha: The Alpha King's Breeder Book 16

Foxed by the Alpha: The Alpha King's Breeder Book 17

The Alpha King's Breeder Books 1-3

Wolf Shifter Fairy Tale Retellings series

Beauty and the Alpha Beast: A Beauty and the Beast Retelling (free!)

Sleeping Beasty : A Sleeping Beauty Retelling

Tangling With the Alpha: A Rapunzel Retelling

Slipping Away From the Alpha: A Cinderella Retelling

Snow White and the Seven Rogues: A Snow White Retelling

The Luna's Vampire Prince series:

The Culling (free!)

The Kingdom

The Conquered

Pregnant With Four Alphas' Babies

Chosen As the Breeder (free!)

Mated to Four Alphas

Threats Against the Breeder

At War for the Breeder

The Stolen Breeder

Four Alphas, Four Babies

Becoming the Luna Queen

Descendants of the Breeder

Desired by the Devil series

Whispers of the Devil (free!)

Banter of the Devil

Murmurs of the Devil

The Mafia Kings series

Indebted to the Mafia King (free!)

<u>Loved by the Mafia King</u>

Claimed by the Mafia King

Secrets of the Mafia King

Burned by the Mafia King

Kidnapped by the Mafia King

Dark Stalker Romance series

Tempted by Sin

Fated to Sin

Secret Billionaires series

Finding the Secret Billionaire by Olivia Bhelle Kildare

Falling for My Secret Billionaire by Bella Moondragon

Driven by the Secret Billionaire by ID Johnson

Wolf Shifter Alpha Kings series

Ravens and Ruins (free!)

Sundrops and Shadows

Snowflakes and Sabotage

Waves and Wickedness

Breezes and Bodies

The Vampire King's Feeder series

Claiming the Alpha's Daughter (free!)

Loving the Alpha's Daughter

Finding the Alpha's Daughter

Bewitching by the Alpha's Son

Writing as B. Moon

The Boy Who Died

Sign up for Bella's newsletter here.

Or get a free novella from The Alpha King's Breeder series when you sign up here:
The Beta and the Maid

Follow Bella on Facebook here.

Follow Bella on Bookbub here.

www.ingramcontent.com/pod-product-compliance
Lightning Source LLC
Chambersburg PA
CBHW060319310726
48976CB00007B/2378